EMBER

EMBER

THE FAIRHAVEN CHRONICLES BOOK THREE

MARTHA CARR

MICHAEL ANDERLE

DISRUPTIVE IMAGINATION

LMBPN Publishing
PMB 196, 2540 South Maryland Pkwy
Las Vegas, NV 89109

First US edition, November 2017
Version 2.02 January 2021
Print ISBN: 978-1-64202-800-3

EMBER TEAM

Thanks to the JIT Readers

Daniel Weigert
Jed Moulton
Kimberly Boyer
Larry Omans
Thomas Ogden
Paul Westman
Micky Cocker
Joshua Ahles
Tim Bischoff

If I've missed anyone, please let me know!

Editor
Lynne Stiegler

DEDICATIONS

From Martha

To everyone who still believes in magic and all the possibilities that holds. To all the readers who make this ride so much fun. And to all the readers just like me who create wonder, big and small, every day.

From Michael

To Family, Friends and
Those Who Love
To Read.
May We All Enjoy Grace
To Live The Life We Are
Called.

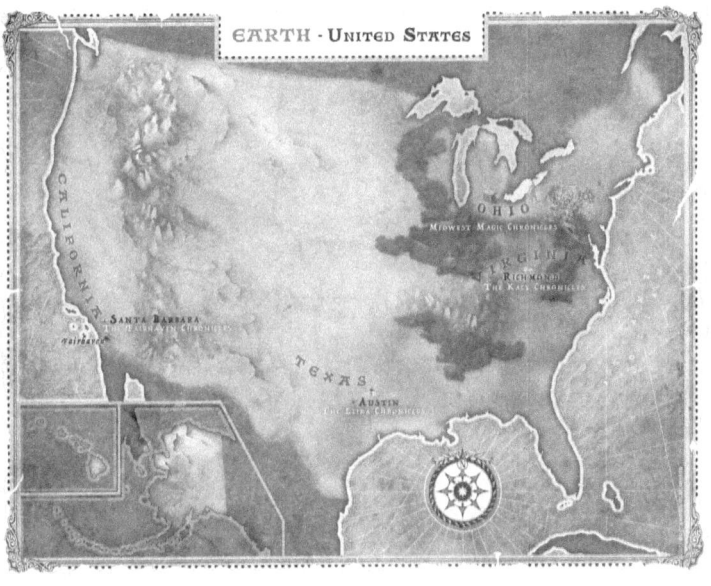

EARTH · United States

CALIFORNIA

OHIO
Midwest Magic Chronicles

VIRGINIA
Richmond
The Kate Chronicles

Santa Barbara

California

TEXAS
Austin
The Links Chronicles

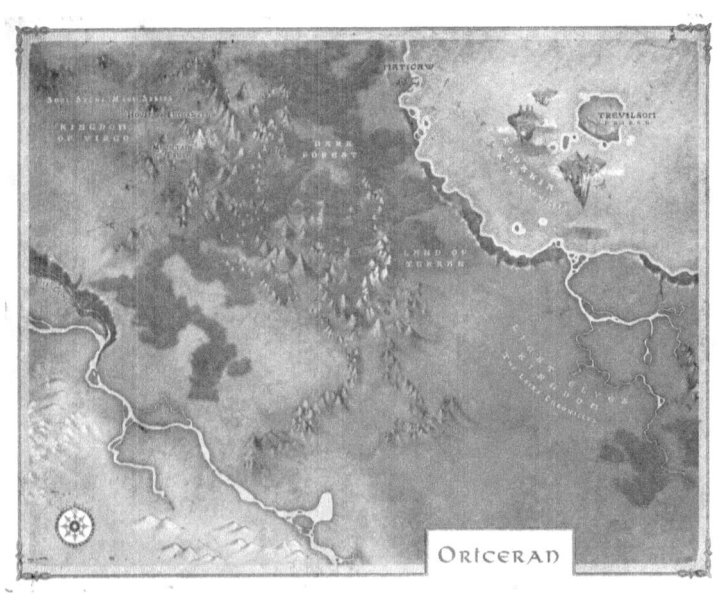

ORICERAN

CHAPTER ONE

In the basement beneath her new Fairhaven home, Victoria Brie widened her stance and focused her energy on the blade in her hands. A dusty beam of sunlight glinted along its sharp edges, and she relished its deadly power. It could slice through paper, skin, bricks—anything.

And it was hers.

The sword's magic pulsed through her, summoned from the powerful artifact embedded in her arm. She swung, the dark magic in her blood sharpening the blade as she practiced. She sliced open invisible foes as she lunged around her basement gym in what would have been a deadly dance if she'd had a real opponent.

The blade cut through the air near her face, and she smirked at the delightful hiss. Eyes closed, breath steady, she could sense everything in the room around her: the punching bag hanging from a support beam, the weights in the corner, the drag of her boots in the dirt, kicking up dust with every step. The rusty musk of the soil filled her lungs, bringing her into the moment.

"You're getting better," a man said.

"Gah!" Startled, nervous, and a little pissed off at the interruption, Victoria tripped. The magical sword disappeared in a puff as she landed hard on her palms and knees.

Shiloh rested against the far wall, arms crossed as he leaned against the stone for support. He lifted a lazy eyebrow as she studied him.

Stupid ghost elf. He might be tied to her Rhazdon Artifact, but she didn't like the way he hovered—mostly invisibly—over her shoulder at all times. He saw everything she did, and likely sensed how she felt.

It freaked her out.

As she stood, she dusted the dirt off her pants. "I told you not to pop up randomly like that. It—wait, did you just compliment me?"

"I did."

"But... But you don't say nice things." They had been together since the day she fused with the Rhazdon Artifact, but she couldn't recall a single kind word ever coming out of his mouth. The bored ghost didn't help, and rarely bothered to show his face at all.

This niceness thing was...well, weird.

He shrugged. "You actually stand a chance of surviving. I'm surprised."

"Uh, thanks?" she said, not sure if that counted as a kindness.

As fast as he had appeared, he vanished. This was his thing, of course. She tried not to let it bother her, especially since she had no control over him. Like it or not, he was connected to her until the day she died.

Yippee.

Hands on her hips, Victoria studied the dusty gym in their hastily acquired new home. Bertha had found it mere hours after she and Audrey had returned from Atlantis to find a new regime slowly encroaching on Fairhaven. The shift in power was led by none other than Luak.

That asshole.

Anger, hatred, and loss burned inside her like a revenge cocktail. He had taken her parents from her, which had jumpstarted this new life in Fairhaven. While she loved her new home, she would give anything to have her parents back.

But even in the powerful underground city of ogres and elves and wizard kings, some things were still impossible.

If Victoria ever stepped outside, Luak and his goons would come for her. Spies now roamed the city, popping up in every alley and peeking through every window.

Nowhere was safe.

Fairhaven lived in fear. The streets were empty, and many shops had closed, their owners fleeing in the night. War was coming, and the final battle for Fairhaven was going to be a bloody one.

Someday she would slit Luak's throat for killing her parents and threatening her new home. She would enjoy watching him bleed out, and, deep down she hoped he would beg for the mercy he wasn't worthy to receive.

Was that cruel of her? Maybe, but her hatred of the elf was well earned. He would die, and she would be the one to kill him.

But today was not that day.

She wasn't ready, and wouldn't be until she was physically strong enough to summon both a sword and a shield at the same time. This Rhazdon Artifact wasn't designed for humans. They simply couldn't develop the necessary strength to wield it properly.

Damn it.

She sighed and trotted up the stairs, debating if she should eat the healthy food Bertha had prepared or throw herself a pity party of one and indulge in some carbo-load binging.

The door to the upstairs hall creaked as she pushed it open, but the tense silence in the kitchen plucked on her nerves like fingers on guitar strings.

Hair on end, shoulders tense, she listened. This dusty old three-story house set her on edge. It had been abandoned for years, and something about it felt wrong. Busy, even when she was alone. Loud, even when no one was talking. Her ears always rang as though someone had just shouted right by her head, even though no one had spoken a word. It was as though someone were always walking past her even when there wasn't a soul around.

But this tension here and now—this was different.

In the kitchen not far away, a chair scraped against the floor. Someone huffed, and the clunk of a mug hitting the table followed. Audrey was training with Bertha today, so it didn't make sense for anyone to be home. Besides, from what little noise the stranger made, he sounded male.

Victoria summoned her sword. It blinked to life, and its familiar weight pressed into her palms. Though it was a deadly blade by nature, she willed it to be even sharper as she stalked toward her prey. Back arched, she tiptoed to the corner as she prepared herself for a fight.

If Luak had come for her, she would give him the fight of his life.

She held her breath as adrenaline pumped through her, sweat pooling on her brow as her fight or flight response kicked in.

Victoria would obviously choose "fight."

Slow, steady, and ready for battle, Victoria peeked around the corner to see who was sitting at her kitchen table. The cloaked form leaned over a plate and adjusted himself in his chair, his familiar white hair hanging down his back as he chewed.

She let out the breath she was holding and nearly kicked the wall. It was Fyrn-freaking-Folly.

Victoria relaxed, her relief tainted with a hint of disappointment at not getting to tear into her arch enemy. At least her mentor was finally home. "I'm glad you're back. It's been weeks. How was it, doing the mighty USA's bidding?"

"Perfectly horrible." The old wizard didn't even bother turning around.

"Did you smack around the asshole who blackmailed you into running their little errand?" She pulled out the chair at the head of the table and sat, elbows resting on the surface as she examined the wizard who had illegally—but to her gratitude—taught her to control her Rhazdon Artifact.

He slouched as he bit into one of the hard-boiled eggs from her fridge, frowning with every bite. "Unfortunately there was no 'smacking around' of anyone, much less the blackmailer. The coward hid halfway around the world. I couldn't even speak to him."

"What a jackass."

Fyrn's eyes landed lazily on her, and his face showed a twinge of displeasure and the barest hint of amusement. "Indeed he was. You've become so eloquent in your time among the magic folk."

Victoria shrugged it off. "I don't pretend to be perfect. Besides, aren't people who cuss supposed to be more honest?"

The wizard rolled his eyes and Victoria suppressed a smirk. The rolling of eyes was her thing, never his. Her habits must have rubbed off on him without his even knowing. He picked up another hardboiled egg and dipped it in the salt piled on his plate. "I sent fairies to find him. I'll speak with him eventually."

"Good. Can't have government folks interfering with Fairhaven."

Fyrn nodded. "We'll resume your training tomorrow. Right now I need a nap."

"Then why did you come here? Did you come to my house just to eat my food?"

"Pretty much."

Victoria chuckled and shook her head, but it wouldn't help to argue. "How did you even find me? Bertha hid us well."

"I know almost everything about Fairhaven, Victoria, and my spies tell me the rest."

Right, the fairies.

"Glad you're on my side, then," Victoria said.

Fyrn smiled and stood, leaving his plate on the table. "As am I."

With that, the old wizard shuffled out of her kitchen

toward the secret passage hidden behind a bookshelf in the back room. The creaky old door hid a dirt path that sloped downward toward the tunnels beneath Fairhaven. They served as the only safe means of traveling unde-tected through the city, despite the plethora of venomous, poisonous, and downright dangerous creatures who lived there.

Fyrn disappeared through the doorway between the kitchen and the living room, the shadows in the chilly home engulfing him until all Victoria could perceive was the subtle tap of his staff hitting the ground as he walked.

"Kooky old fart," she muttered to herself.

"I heard that," he shouted from the passage.

Victoria groaned. He really did know everything.

Fyrn had a difficult choice to make.

He wandered the tunnels beneath Victoria's new house, in no hurry to return home. Though he enjoyed the idea of stretching out in his bed and sleeping until he no longer could, he had a life or death dilemma on his hands.

Victoria.

He had exhausted every resource, used every favor, and read every book on the subject. All that effort, and still he had no answers. Much to his disappointment, he was no closer to finding a way to strengthen her body through magic.

No spell, no ritual, no relic in existence could give her enough physical strength to completely master her Rhazdon Artifact. And if she didn't—if she couldn't wield both her sword and shield at once—Luak would kill her in their inevitable battle.

"Hello, sir," a squeaky little voice said from the shadows of the tunnel.

He smiled despite himself. "Hello, my dear Melzzie. How were things while I was gone?"

The little fairy with the long fire-red hair flew into view, her tiny wings buzzing as she hovered by his head. "Things in Fairhaven are horrendous. No one has seen King Bornt in weeks. Many think he's in prison, or dead. No one loved our king, but he was the lesser of two evils in this situation. There are some who believe Luak has already taken over. Some say he's biding his time until he has enough forces to enslave the city."

"He hasn't taken over—not yet. But he will."

Melzzie shivered. "What terrible times."

"We still have hope."

"The Rhazdon host?"

Fyrn nodded.

"But Luak is a menace. He has two Rhazdon Artifacts, sir, maybe more. It's impossible to beat him."

"It is, isn't it?" Fyrn replied wistfully, eyes glazing as his feet led him home out of habit. He had walked these tunnels since his youth, and nothing that lived here scared him in the slightest. The monsters here seemed to know he was a force to be reckoned with, and they kept a respectful distance.

The monsters in the bowels of Fairhaven might not have scared him, but losing Victoria to a savage elf? Now, that sent dread clear to his toes. She had grown into her power while protecting and cherishing the city that had served as her safe haven from the storm of her loss, pain, and grief.

"These are indeed desperate times," he muttered.

The fairy flitted overhead, her tiny blue wings buzzing. "I know the Rhazdon host is powerful, but can she truly defeat Luak and his mercenaries? He's building an army, Fyrn, with a rich woman's gold."

"He is, and it will not be easy to stop him. It will take time to find out who his mistress is, but that's not urgent. Saving Fairhaven is. We don't have the luxury of waiting for more information or an opportune moment. If we don't act soon, we'll lose our chance forever."

"Forever? But why?"

Fyrn rubbed his neck, hating to admit the truth. "If Luak takes over and too many of his soldiers come here, we will never reclaim our city. He will be too powerful, the castle impenetrable, and his influence too hard to shake. He will own the criminal elements of the city, and will bargain with them to keep Fairhaven in chaos. Hell, it's already happening. We lose more citizens every night, whether it's someone escaping in the darkness to a better life or a mugging gone wrong."

"What can we do?" The terrified fairy wrung her hands, biting her lip as she waited for an answer.

Fyrn didn't like it, but they had only one option at this point. "To kill him, Victoria will need to be able to win a fight with impossible odds. It can't matter if she's outnumbered. She must always win. Unfortunately, Bertha tells me Victoria lost to the Atlanteans in a surprise attack. That can never happen again."

"A surprise attack?"

He shook his head. "Losing. It can't matter what she's faced with. She must always win."

"But how?" Melzzie asked.

Fyrn knew. He simply didn't like the answer. "Melzzie, have you found that Rhazdon Artifact I asked for before I left?"

"Not yet, sir. Wherever it is, it's very well hidden. We have a few leads, but nothing certain."

Fyrn sighed in disappointment. "I'm not surprised, but it's imperative that we find it as soon as possible. Fetch the others. Leave only the essential spies in the palace and Drefus' den. Everyone else must hunt for it."

"But sir, another Rhazdon Artifact? What if... What if she..." The fairy didn't need to finish her sentence. Both she and Fyrn knew the risks. Victoria's good heart could become corrupted by the sheer power blistering through her veins. It wouldn't be a matter of losing control of herself, but of essentially slipping into the darkness and embracing cruelty and pain like so many other Rhazdon hosts before her.

Dark magic twisted even good people, and that was Fyrn's ultimate fear. In her effort to gain enough power to protect those she loved, Victoria could step too far into the shadows. She'd slowly begin to indulge in bloodlust and develop a thirst for control over others.

In effect, she would become the next Luak—only she would not stoop so low as to have a master.

Fyrn shook his head, doing his best to clear his mind of fear. It slowed him down, and served no real purpose. He had faith in her good nature and her pure heart, even if she did curse like a sailor.

"We have no choice, Melzzie." Fyrn hated to speak those words, but in this case they were the truth. Either Victoria enhanced her skills with another Rhazdon Artifact, or Fairhaven and Victoria both would fall to Luak. Fyrn was a powerful wizard, but his magic had limits that fell short of fighting a full army and a bloodthirsty elf with seemingly unlimited resources.

Only Victoria could save them, and she would pay the cost for her power.

He sighed, pausing in the middle of the tunnel to lean on his staff. If he had second thoughts, now was the time to stop this madness.

Now or never.

"You remember what the Rhazdon Artifact looks like? The onyx bear figurine?" he softly asked the fairy.

She nodded, but she frowned shortly thereafter.

Fyrn knew that look. "You doubt my decision."

"You know best, sir. It's just…"

"Yes?"

"We've been talking, the other fairies and I. King Bornt won't be happy to hear she's willingly hunting for a second Rhazdon Artifact. The first one was a mistake, but to actively seek a second one?"

He sighed, at a loss. "I know, Melzzie. I know. They're still illegal, after all, and her means of acquiring the first one was unconventional at best. Accidents happen, but *deliberately* merging with more dark magic could undo the fragile public image Victoria has built here in Fairhaven."

The little fairy nodded. "I'm trying to be realistic, sir, and look at this from every angle like you taught me. Even if she saves the city, people will fear her. Some may rally against her, already spooked by the power-mad elf who is trying to take over. Some may think she's nothing more than an opportunist who will use the chaos to take the throne for herself. Even if she wins the battle, she will likely face more wars on the other side."

"Yes, she may."

The tiny fairy began to fly in circles around his head, her version of pacing. "Fear means assumptions, and assumptions about powerful people can lead to panic and riots. The people will fear her, even if she saves them."

"They might love her."

"A Rhazdon host with two artifacts?" The fairy raised one delicate eyebrow in doubt.

Fyrn shrugged. "It's possible."

"Perhaps, but it's unlikely."

"Our options are to save Fairhaven with dark magic or let it fall to a murderer. Her public image taking a hit is an acceptable risk."

"Even if that risk puts her life in danger?"

He stared at the ground, trying to ignore the sadness tugging at his heart. "I'll do everything in my power to keep that from happening, but yes. Even then."

Melzzie set her hands on her hips as her wings buzzed, suspending her in midair. "Very well, sir. If you're certain?"

"I am."

"I will need your help then, sir. From what we have discovered, it's impossible to find. The one you want has been lost for centuries. Is it our only choice?"

"It's not lost, it's hidden. And we have no other option but to find it. It's the only Rhazdon Artifact of its kind."

She snapped her tiny jaw shut and nodded, face set with determination. "Right away, sir."

The fairy flitted off the way she had come, no doubt to rally the others. His hundreds of fairies were well worth the cost of keeping them fed and happy, and he was grateful for their loyalty. When others failed, they always came through.

They would find the bear figurine, and when they did he wouldn't delay. Victoria wouldn't refuse his request. In fact, this had been her idea originally.

That worried him most of all.

CHAPTER TWO

A udrey splashed water on her face, savoring the icy chill of the droplets when a few snuck down her neck. They washed away the sweat of a hard day, and she inhaled sharply to fully savor the sensation. The day's training had left her famished, and she could almost taste the apples in the feed bag by the back door of Bertha's shop.

She reached for one of the red fruits, but a thundering voice behind her made her jump. "What do you think you're doing, child?"

"Eating an apple," Audrey said, fingers poised to grab one.

The ogre crossed the gap between them and smacked her hand. "You ridiculous humans. This fruit isn't fit for consumption. It's feed for the cattle! Honestly, you'd think you and Victoria were raised in a barn."

"But—"

"Nonsense," Bertha said, cutting her off.

"I just—"

"I'll make you some proper food, child. Now go wash up in the restroom and give me space to work."

"Fine, you win." Audrey chuckled and shook her head. She would grab one later when Bertha wasn't looking. The uniform hatred of apples in Fairhaven made her wonder if any of these people had been brave enough to try the sweet fruits.

Wild guess: Nope.

Audrey trotted up the thin stairway that ran up the back wall of the house, tracing the familiar steps she and Victoria had taken every day when they lived here. The floorboards creaked louder than before beneath her feet.

Still sweaty from her sword training with Bertha, Audrey shut the bathroom door behind herself and rested for a moment. A white clawfoot tub big enough for three humans was set against the far wall beneath the window, and a simple sink with a large mirror above it pressed against the wall to her right. She went to it and leaned her palms on the basin, staring at her reflection while she caught her breath.

Damn, she was pretty.

The effects of her time in Atlantis hadn't worn off. Her skin still shimmered, and her silken hair had naturally soft curls that had never been there before. But more beautiful even than that was the tiara still sitting on her head. The thin silver band curved along her forehead and ended in the shimmering crystal point, prominent and stunning.

She couldn't take it off, since the act of removing it would kill her. That, at least, she shared with Victoria. They were marked for life, stuck forever with the dark magic in their blood.

Calling it "dark magic" is a little harsh, a soft voice said in her ear.

In the mirror's reflection, a large blue koi hovered behind her as though it were swimming through the air. Its magnificent fins shimmered and rippled like waves in a pond, and it nudged her shoulder. A cool tingle burst through her at its touch, and she looked over her shoulder.

At nothing.

The koi existed only in reflections and Audrey's mind. Unlike Shiloh, no one could see the water spirit tied to Audrey's Atlantean Artifact. It was striking how similar the two types of magical artifacts were, and yet so unique from each other at the same time.

"Sorry, you're not evil," Audrey said with a smile to the koi in the mirror.

The corner of its mouth tilted slightly upward in its own version of a smile. *We should practice.*

Right, with the power her tiara gave her, which was shape-shifting. "Right now?"

Masters become masters because they practice in the little moments. Every pause, every moment to yourself is an opportunity to try again. Every tiny shift matters, and the more you practice, the better you will become. Besides, if not now, when?

Audrey frowned. It never was a good time, of course, especially when every shift reminded her of Atlantis. Of a home she had lost. Of a people who had loved her, but had tried to kill her dearest friend in the world.

They are not here, little one. Only I am, and I will never hurt you.

Audrey smiled in gratitude. "Okay, how do I do this? How do I change shape?"

Start small, the koi said.

"Just a few shifts, though. Bertha's waiting."

As you wish, little one.

As the koi had taught her in the few quiet moments they'd had together so far, Audrey cleared her mind and took one deep, slow breath. She focused on something minor—her hair color. It was time to try something starkly different.

"Let's go for blonde," she said.

Her roots began to shimmer on cue, and the black faded. Her silky hair turned the color of corn, strand by strand. The shade slowly crept to the tips, and she couldn't help but smile at her success.

As her black locks faded to gold, her mind wandered back to Atlantis. She remembered General Cato, now dead, shoving her against a wall and threatening her friends' lives. She remembered the king's warm welcome, and his stark shift into the cold and heartless man who had later apathetically admitted to brainwashing her. She remembered target practice in the garden, and the dazzling way Atlantean light glinted off their crystal-clear ponds.

All at once she realized Atlantis was both a home and a prison.

Her focus destroyed, the golden color slowly crept back to her roots until it was completely gone. "Damn."

Very good. You will soon learn to hold your shifts even when you're not completely focused. Give it time.

"Thanks," Audrey said with a relieved smile.

One more.

Audrey's eyes fell to her chest, and she grinned mischievously. "Time for bigger boobs."

The koi chuckled. The melodic sound was distorted a bit, almost like water rushing over pebbles in a brook.

Biting her lip in concentration, Audrey narrowed her eyes as her breasts began to push against the corset atop her white blouse. Weight pulled at her chest, and she frowned as a twinge of pain shot down her back.

She blinked herself out of the shift and her breasts returned to their normal size. "Scratch that. Big boobs kill my back. Why are we women supposed to want huge breasts? It just hurts."

As you master your shifts, you will discover many afflictions that befall our fellow creatures. You can become an ogre, an elf, a witch...whatever you desire, but you will feel their pain as well.

"If I morph into a witch, can I use their magic?"

It is possible, yes. When you shift, you take on the abilities of that race. That is one of the reasons your tiara is so coveted, and one of the reasons you need to fiercely guard it.

"Well, that, and I'll die if anyone steals it from me."

That, too. The koi smiled again. *However, bear in mind that wizardly magic takes decades to master. I would be cautious of how and when you use it. I know you can achieve great things with your new powers, Audrey, but the key is to move slowly and trust yourself. Why, I even saw a past master become a snarx.*

Audrey quirked an eyebrow. "No joke? A snarx? Fun!"

The koi nodded. *She was ferocious and magnificent. None dared oppose her. In the end, her greed destroyed her.*

Oh. Less fun.

Something the water spirit had said struck a chord deep within Audrey. "Wait, you think I'm your master?"

You wear the tiara, so you are my master.

"I don't know if I'm comfortable with that."

The koi chuckled again. *You are a sweet soul, Audrey Xavier.*

"Literally no one has ever said that about me. I'm always the asshole in the group."

Is that who you want to be?

Audrey frowned, not entirely sure of the answer. "Let's save the philosophical shit for another day. In the meantime, there's an apple with my name on it."

Victoria might enjoy one as well.

A twinge of guilt stopped her in her tracks. "I hadn't even thought to get her one."

The Atlantean gene is hard to ignore.

It certainly was. The selfish impulses sometimes drowned all other thoughts. She might have stifled the Atlantean voice in her head when she'd had her epiphany back in Atlantis, but it hadn't died.

The repressed voice seemed to still call the shots in subtle ways, like not holding the door for people, always getting herself food first, or not sharing when she grabbed a snack from the kitchen. These were small and silent changes, but noticeable nonetheless.

But Victoria was an honorary Atlantean. Family. And to an Atlantean, family came first. She wasn't sure she would ever tell her parents about their heritage. Hell, they probably wouldn't believe her. Legally she wasn't allowed to tell them at all, so maybe it was for the best. She didn't want to drag them into something they didn't want to be a part of.

Despite the many assholes who lived in her long-lost magical city, Audrey missed Atlantis. Its beauty, its food… even the dresses. Everything there had shimmered. She had given up the throne to return with Victoria, and if they hadn't tried to kill her best friend, Audrey might have even gone back to visit.

Screw Atlantis. Screw the king. Screw General Cato—though since he had wanted to marry her in a bid to get the kingdom for himself, screwing the general might very well have been in her future had she not escaped. She grimaced. He wasn't exactly her type.

Besides, she had her crystals. She had her tiara. Audrey finally had power, *real* power she could use to defend those she loved.

With a sigh Audrey flipped on the faucet, and water magically sprang from the tap. She didn't understand Fairhaven plumbing, but in the end it didn't matter. She just wanted water, not a logistics lesson.

Her mind still wandered. Victoria had believed in her when everyone else had assumed she would go rogue and lose herself to Atlantis. Therefore, Audrey would do everything in her power to prove her friend right.

CHAPTER THREE

"**K***eep your elbows in*, damn it!"
Victoria huffed as she dodged one of Fyrn's famous combos. They were deep in one of the dozens of training caves they had begun to use. For safety, they never went to the same one twice in a two-month span, and always randomized their choices.

Three blasts of purple light sailed toward her, the last in a staggering twelve-shot combo he had aimed at her head. So far she had dodged them all, but the final few were always the hardest. Besides, when she *did* manage to dodge all the attacks in a combo, he just shot more at her.

Styx flitted overhead, the pixie cheering each time she avoided a blow from her mentor. He kept safely out of reach, a lesson he had learned last week after a scorched wing and much melodramatic sobbing.

After the last bolt passed Victoria wiped the sweat from her brow and tensed, not allowing herself to relish the victory of dodging all of Fyrn's attacks. Any time she did, he shot one at her face.

Those *hurt.*

She readied herself for the next attack, but it didn't come.

Fyrn paused by the entrance to the dark cave, which was lit only by the dozens of floating flames he had cast around its edges. In the flickering shadows Victoria couldn't make out what he was doing. It looked like he was just staring at the wall.

"I see. Thank you," he eventually said. With that, a small shadow darted away from his head and back into the dark tunnel.

Ah. One of his fairy spies had come to pay him a visit.

"That's all for today," the old wizard said.

"What? We've only been going for a few hours. You never call it quits this early."

"Something requires my attention. I must do some research. Take the rest of the evening off, but remember— no Berserk. No public appearances."

"Yeah, yeah." She kicked the cave floor, disappointed. Fairhaven was home to her favorite game in the world, and she couldn't even play it without the looming risk of death.

It seemed "looming risk of death" was part of her job description now.

"Victoria, you will arrive at my cottage tomorrow at sunrise through the secret passage in my office. We will have much to discuss." With that, the old wizard shuffled into the dark tunnel, the receding clicks of his staff on the rocky ground the only indication of which direction he had taken.

Victoria hesitated in the cave. A day off, and all because Fyrn had to do some vague research about something he wouldn't discuss. With Luak overtaking the city bit by bit and the increasing reports of death and murder in her beloved city, Fyrn had ordered longer training sessions and harder workouts. And suddenly he had *research* to do?

"What the hell just happened?" she asked herself.

Styx landed on her shoulder and shrugged, muttering something in his own language. He was apparently as befuddled as her.

Victoria summoned her sword and stabbed one of the hovering flames as Fyrn had taught her not long ago. The charmed fire clung to her blade, and she brandished the duo like a torch. The fire cast dancing shadows on the cave walls as she retraced her steps toward home.

Without warning, the hair on her neck stood on end. The sensation of being watched set her nerves on fire, and she paused to strain her ears. Nothing but the drip of water could be heard, but she remained still. It would only take one clue to indicate what had joined her: a breath, a scuffle, or maybe a claw scraping along the rock.

But no clues came. Only silence.

Even though she had spent a considerable amount of time down here, there were still deadly—and very hungry—creatures in these caves.

While they might not faze Fyrn, *she* didn't want to run into any of them.

Alert, nervous, and ready to fight, Victoria headed homeward.

When Victoria reached their hideaway, she made sure to double-check the lock after the door closed behind her. Whatever had been watching her had stuck with her until the Main Street tunnels, where she had lost it in the labyrinth.

Even though it hadn't followed her all the way back, she didn't like the idea of someone—or something—knowing where she lived.

She trotted up the stairs to the kitchen, eager for a bite to eat, and found Audrey at the table. As Victoria approached, Audrey fanned out a deck of cards and cooled herself with it. "Fancy a game of Mittle?"

"What the ever-loving fuck is Mittle?"

"I have no idea."

With a smile, Victoria picked out one of the cards from the fan. A strange circular symbol glowed brilliant blue on a white background.

Audrey snatched it back and shoved it into the deck. "Bertha gave me this today. Let's figure out how to play it."

Victoria reached into the magically chilled fridge for some cheese and cool water. "Did it come with rules?"

"Are you joking? Of course not. This city is all about baptism by fire."

Laughing, Victoria plopped at the table. "Lay it on me. I could use a distraction."

"Something follow you home again?"

Victoria's smile faded, and she bit into the cheese to keep from answering. Since she and Audrey could communicate simply by gesture, she was pretty sure she didn't need to say a word. Audrey already knew.

Her friend cleared her throat. "Right. Sorry. Mittle. The game of cards with weird symbols I don't understand."

Audrey spread the cards on the table. They had sigils and marks Victoria had never seen in her life. Some of them glowed, pulsating as they lay on top of other cards.

"Jesus, where do we start?" Victoria touched one of the glowing cards and a small puff of smoke billowed from the symbol.

Audrey laughed. "Seriously, what on Earth is this? How do we play?"

"Fuck it. Let's play 'Go Fish.'"

With a grin, Audrey grabbed the cards and shuffled. As she did, occasional puffs of smoke came from the deck. She shook her head. "Something tells me this is the one deck of cards in the world that won't work for Go Fish."

"That's what makes it fun."

Audrey dealt them a handful of cards each and set the deck between them. Victoria kicked up her feet and examined her hand, eyes scanning the myriad confusing symbols. None matched exactly, but several were close enough that she wondered if they should count. The last one, tucked behind the others, glowed pink. "Have any glowing pink circles?"

"I…uh…no?"

Victoria stared Audrey over the tops of her cards, challenging her friend. "You sure about that?"

"They're *all* circles! Do they glow at different times? Do they change colors? I don't know these things!"

Victoria laughed and threw the cards on the table. "Checkmate! I win!"

"That doesn't even—"

"It's Fairhaven. Nothing has to make sense."

Audrey chuckled and tossed her cards on the table too. "Eh, whatever. We got to hang out a bit, and that's what matters."

"Maybe we should make friends with someone who knows how to play this game."

"I bet Bertha would come over. She might be stuck here soon anyway. She wants to keep her shop open as long as possible, before..." Audrey fidgeted in her chair. Neither had to finish the sentence.

Bertha wanted to keep her shop open to feed those in town who were hungry and couldn't leave, and she would do so until Luak came to kill her. Then, and only then, would she sneak away from the store she loved.

The fun of their stupid little game evaporated as harsh reality sank in.

They were prisoners here, under constant threat from a deranged madman who wanted to murder Victoria for her Rhazdon Artifact and slit Audrey's throat for fun. They knew few who could be trusted. One step outside meant Luak would find them, one way or another.

"I hate keeping to the tunnels," Audrey said softly.

Victoria nodded. "Me, too, but it won't be for much longer. Luak is mine. I'm so close, Audrey. I can taste it."

"Do you think it's true? Is the king dead?"

Victoria tapped a finger on the table, chewing her lip as she thought. "I do. There's no reason for Luak to keep him alive. No one here likes or respects him, and he's not exactly charismatic or powerful. No one feels like he keeps them safe. I mean, think about it as objectively as you can. What benefit would Luak get by keeping the king alive?"

"The sick pleasure of torturing him?"

Victoria grimaced and sank farther into her seat. "I hadn't thought about that."

"Probably a good thing. Don't let your mind go there unless you have to."

Victoria sighed. "I know it sounds awful, but maybe it's not the worst thing if he's gone. Maybe it's time for a democracy here. If he's dead, maybe we can make something better once we get rid of Luak."

Audrey smiled, and it warmed Victoria's heart. They had been through so much, not just in Fairhaven but throughout their lives. At every step, Audrey had been there. She was dependable and reliable, and she would always have Victoria's back.

But even better than that, Audrey seemed truly happy. Despite having discovered she wasn't fully human and having nearly been brainwashed by a corrupt monarchy, Audrey looked...well, at home. Peaceful.

Happy.

Victoria lifted her fist in a gesture they hadn't shared in a while. "To the end?"

"To the end, V," Audrey said, bumping her fist against Victoria's.

Through blood, scars, and shattered bones, she and Audrey would be together to the end, no matter what came their way. And that, at least, gave Victoria a sense of comfort amidst all the crazy.

CHAPTER FOUR

B right and early the next morning, Victoria stood in
Fyrn's messy office. Styx had decided to stay at the
house and gorge himself on the oranges Bertha had
brought over, and Victoria couldn't blame him. The pixie
deserved a break.

As Victoria exited from the tunnels beneath Fyrn's
house through the secret bookcase, she stepped around a
pile of books set on the floor. One of the tomes lay open to
a page covered with a thick layer of dust, and the room was
littered with similar piles of red and gold books. The stale
air reminded her of a crypt, and as she passed the desk she
disturbed one of the dozens of loose papers lying on the
surface.

It must have been some form of *organized* chaos, but she
was leaning more toward just chaos.

A golden ray of light broke through the window behind
her, illuminating the door. Out of self-preservation she
knocked before emerging, lest she be blown to bits by a
surprised wizard who hadn't yet had his coffee. As soon as

her knuckles rapped the wood the door swung outward into the hallway, and a plume of dust mushroomed into the sunshine.

In the dark hall, a silhouette slipped around a corner with the familiar *tap, tap, tap* on the hardwood, the form moving toward the living room.

Victoria coughed. "Fyrn, you need to dust your house at least once a decade."

"Come in, already," he muttered from another room.

Careful to step around even more books littered all over the floor and leaning against the walls, Victoria eventually found her way to the couch and plopped down. Another plume of dust shot into the air, and she favored her mentor with a mild glare. "At least hire a maid."

"Waste of money. Besides, I don't like entertaining company. A mess means they leave faster." He waved away the thought with a flick of his wrist and sank into the armchair across from her. His cane stood upright beside his chair as though held by an invisible hand.

She rested her head on one fist, waiting. He likely didn't want to talk about his lack of a social life, but she couldn't for the life of her think of what he *did* want to discuss with her.

Fyrn made himself comfortable while he searched for words, often pausing to stroke his beard or lean back against the overstuffed armchair's cushions. For several moments, neither spoke.

Victoria tapped her finger against the side of her jaw, a little baffled by the silence. With every second that passed she became a bit more worried. Perhaps he wanted to stop training. Perhaps he wanted her to leave Fairhaven.

Whatever he wanted to explore with her, it seemed as though he couldn't quite bring himself to start the conversation. And, since Fyrn was used to yelling obscenities at her and hitting her with things, that was a very bad sign.

He finally looked straight at her and searched her face for several minutes before he broke the silence. "Victoria, what is your purpose?"

"To kill Luak."

He sighed. "Beyond that."

"Right now that's all I can think about."

His jaw tensed, and she had the feeling she had given the wrong answer. It was, however, the truth.

At least... Well, it had been before she thought more about it.

She hesitated, mind wandering through the months since she had come home to an elf in her living room and watched her father summon a magic sword. The agony of watching her father die. The panic when Luak had tried to kill her, too. The crackle of flames as her family home burned with her still in it. The way she had desperately tried to get upstairs to rescue her mother, only to be dragged out against her will.

A hot tear burned in her eye, and she blinked it away.

The burning hatred for her parents' killer had never subsided, but she couldn't in all honesty say killing him was her only goal in life. Not when she lived here, in this impossibly beautiful city of elves and ogres. Since she had begun to learn about magic, this place had wormed its way into her heart. In fact, it had won it, and become her home.

"And protect Fairhaven," she added.

Fyrn sat almost imperceptibly straighter, and she could

tell her answer piqued his interest. "I'm glad to hear that, Victoria. Revenge will eat you alive, because if—not when —you achieve it, there's nothing left for you in the ashes. After the war, after the fight, after the bloodshed, the anger will still be there unless you have something else to fuel you."

Her shoulders slumped and she sank a bit in her chair as she mulled his words. He had a point. A frustrating, obnoxious point.

"So what is *your* purpose, Victoria Brie?"

This time she waited and listened to her intuition before speaking. As the answer formed in her head, she knew in her heart this was her *real* purpose. Her "why." The one thing that would drive her to train until she bled and then push a bit harder. "My purpose is to do what's right and bring justice to those who need it. To protect Fairhaven from whatever threatens it. And, eventually, to get my revenge on Luak," she added, anger flaring at the mere mention of the bastard's name.

Fyrn nodded. "You will have your day, Victoria. Much sooner than you think."

This caught her attention. She perked up, eager to hear what he had discovered. If she would soon go after Luak, it meant that he had discovered some method of making her physically strong enough to wield both a sword and a shield from her Rhazdon Artifact. With that ability, she would finally master the dark magic swirling in her blood.

The thought alone sent shivers of hope and anticipation down her spine.

The wizard pressed his thin fingers together. "To defeat Luak, you will have to sacrifice everything. Your time, your magic—maybe even your life. Are you prepared to do that? Are you willing to die for what you believe in?"

Victoria hesitated once more, simply to allow her brain to catch up with her mouth. But after she had simmered on the thought, she knew the answer without a doubt. "I am."

"You are what? Be clear. Say it!"

"I'm willing to die to protect Fairhaven. I'm willing to die to kill Luak."

Fyrn's shoulders heaved as he sucked in an uncharacteristically shaky breath. "I ask you in all seriousness, Victoria. I have a plan, and though I will do everything in my power to protect you, you may very well die."

"I'm ready."

He nodded to himself, seemingly content—if not altogether happy—with her answer. "You will receive another Rhazdon Artifact."

"But you said—"

"I know what I said, but there is no other option. Trust me, I've exhausted every possible avenue to make you physically stronger. This is the only choice, and my fairies have located the one you must fuse with."

Victoria leaned back in her chair, processing what he had said. "But you said another might corrupt me. It might make me bloodthirsty and manipulative."

Fyrn rubbed his temples, shoulders hunched. "It *is* a risk, one which originally made me refuse to even consider it. But our options have diminished. Either you augment your Rhazdon Artifact by adding another to your body, or Luak will defeat you. He'll kill you, Victoria, even with your advanced understanding of your dagger. If you face him now, or even in the future, without being able to push past the physical limitations of your human body, you will fail."

"So it's die and lose Fairhaven to a vindictive murderer, or risk becoming one myself?"

"We don't know that the second will corrupt *you*, but we *do* know Luak's Rhazdon Artifacts have corrupted *him*. Fusing you with a second Rhazdon Artifact is the lesser of two evils."

Victoria stared at the floor, lost in thoughts of blood and pain. Fusing with a second Rhazdon Artifact would be agony, but well worth it if it meant she could do what she had come here to do.

Her mind raced back to her childhood home as it went up in flames with her father's body lying in the middle of it all. Her throat clenched, but a realization hit her square in the chest. "For me to fuse with another Rhazdon Artifact, someone has to die."

"You're right," the old wizard said.

"Who? Luak?"

"We need you to be trained and ready to fight Luak with the gifts this Rhazdon Artifact will bestow upon you. So, no. You will have to kill someone or something else."

Victoria stiffened in her chair, the reality of the situation weighing on her like bricks in a backpack. She hesitated, wondering if she could go through with this. "It can't be an innocent."

"It won't be."

"Someone horrible. Someone who deserves it."

"Are you willing to decide who deserves death?"

She caught her mentor's eyes and let the silence fill the

air as she debated how to answer his question. "I don't know."

"You need to find out."

"I will." She nodded, crossing her legs as she stared at the floor, lost in thought again. It was turning out to be a far heavier conversation than she had anticipated, and she wasn't quite sure how to process everything quite yet.

"Victoria?" Fyrn stared at her intently, apparently trying to impress the weight of what he was about to say upon her.

"Yes?"

"We might not stop with two Rhazdon Artifacts."

Her eyebrows shot up her forehead. "What?"

Fyrn nodded, a grim expression on his face. "We might need three, Victoria. Or more. Each could corrupt you, of course, but you're in worse danger than you realize with each new one you acquire. Some of the ghosts attached to them actively try to kill their hosts. Some make their host's life a living hell, either by saying terrible things or merely by how horrifying they look."

"Jesus," she muttered.

The wizard continued, "All this over time could make you as cruel and heartless as Luak if you're not careful, and maybe even if you are. Are you prepared to suffer the consequences that may come with acquiring more power?"

"I'll never be like him."

"The Rhazdon Artifacts are immensely powerful. You don't know what will happen, and you must be prepared. Now answer me."

Her jaw tensed, but she nodded. "To do what's right and

protect Fairhaven, I accept whatever consequences might arise."

"And how will you keep from losing yourself?"

At that, at least, she could smile. "I have you to yell at me."

"Victoria, be serious."

"I am. I have you, Audrey, and even Diesel. I have my Berserk team, the Plits. I have Bertha. The people I love will keep me in line, even if I begin to lose myself. Luak doesn't have that. If he did at one time, they abandoned him when he needed them most. None of you will abandon me."

Fyrn relaxed a bit in his chair, and a thin smile crept across his face. "I'm proud of you, Victoria."

It took everything in her power not to beam with joy. A compliment from Fyrn was like winning the lottery while riding a unicorn. "Thank you."

"Rest today. Prepare. Take care of yourself. Time is not on our side. We don't have long to get everything we need, but you need some personal space to think through everything we have discussed. We will leave after I've made the necessary preparations. This will not be an easy trip, Victoria, and you will have to earn this second Rhazdon Artifact. Are you ready for a grueling journey?"

She nodded and stood, hands balling into fists. "Whatever it takes, you know I'll do it."

The old wizard smiled. "I know."

CHAPTER FIVE

F yrn watched from the second-floor hallway window
as the city slowly came alive. Victoria had long since
snuck through the tunnels to her home, but he stared out
at Fairhaven as if it could somehow save him from what
needed to be done. He had decided against training today,
since she needed to process everything he had told her.

Victoria—through whatever twist of fate had brought
magic into her life—was a Rhazdon host, and was
attracting more and more power. It wouldn't stop, at least
not any time soon. She would acquire more influence,
learn impossible new skills, and put herself in harm's way
each time she found a new Rhazdon Artifact.

As the morning light broke over his beloved city,
Melzzie flitted into his peripheral vision and sat on the
crystal atop his staff. Her tiny legs dangled over its edge,
and she wrung her hands. "Do you think she's going to be
okay?"

He laughed. "I'd be a rich man if I had been paid every

time I heard those words over the years. I don't make rash decisions, Melzzie. Never have. She can do this."

"But are you right? Can she really handle another Rhazdon Artifact? Look what it did to Luak, and so many others before him."

To that, Fyrn had no answer. He simply watched the quiet Fairhaven morning as a few shopkeepers began to open their doors in the distant streets. If he was right, she would resist the evil in whatever Rhazdon Artifact she fused with regardless of its power. If he was right, she would retain the pure heart that had brought her this far.

But Fyrn had been wrong before.

Fork in hand, Luak took the first bite from a perfectly round chocolate cake on the counter in a small suburban home on the outskirts of London. His fork clinked against the crystal platter the cake sat on, the delicate sound the only noise in the massive home.

A corpse was sprawled over the couch, proof that no mortal could run from Luak. He ate the dead man's cake, furious with himself.

There had been humans to greet him, of course, but there had been no Rhazdon Artifact to collect. Not one. No one in this home had even known of Oriceran and magic, much less of the Rhazdon Artifact that was supposed to be here. He had already ransacked the house for the ornate crystal and gold ring, but he had found nothing.

Once again, Luak's sources had been wrong.

Furious at his failure, he grabbed the platter and threw

it against the wall. The fragile crystal shattered, and the dessert splattered on the damask wallpaper. Chocolate goo dripped to the floor.

Pacing the kitchen, Luak ran his hands through his hair to calm himself.

The last four homes had been dry, filled with nothing more than pathetic mortals who gasped and pleaded for a few more seconds of miserable life. His trails were getting cold, and that meant he was out of time.

To remain his master's favorite, he needed to take Fairhaven over. He had already planted the seeds of dissent, and now it was time to harvest what he had sown.

And it had all begun with that stupid girl who had stolen his Rhazdon Artifact. He would bleed her dry for the trouble she had caused him, and he would see to it that every second of her death was pure agony.

CHAPTER SIX

Victoria laughed, her shoulders aching with joy.

After the news from Fyrn she had paced her home like a caged tiger, simultaneously excited and nervous. The pent-up energy had gone to her head. She'd decided she had to play a game of Berserk or she would lose her mind, and since she couldn't leave the tunnels, the Plits had brought the game to her.

And she was having the best damn time of her life.

"Get it, get it!" Victoria pointed toward a hundred-point green fidget. The little indestructible creature curled into a ball and sped off down the tunnel, an emerald blur in a sea of gray. Thankfully the hundred-point fidgets were far easier to spot against the cave floor than on the Berserk field. She felt a little like she was cheating, but this was all in good fun.

The tunnel they had found was perfect for Berserk—as wide as a regular field, with a smooth floor and few boulders or stalagmites to crash into. Barriers at either end blockaded their little game, and Fyrn had cast a magical shield to hide their noise. Magically suspended flames hovered in the air all over the makeshift arena, casting dappled light over the barebones playing field.

It was far from a fair Berserk match, since the green and gold fidgets stood out like sore thumbs. But really, this was all in good fun. Besides, they were a bit harder to spot down here, since a few alcoves and boulders offered hiding spaces the fidgets otherwise wouldn't have had. Still, the lack of exits made it a perfect impromptu arena.

As the green fidget sped past Audrey dove at it, her bare elbow scraping the rocky ground as she pinned the creature. To her credit she barely winced as blood pooled on her skin, and she held it tightly. "Edgar!"

"On my way!" the big ogre shouted. The ground shook beneath him as he charged toward her and reached for the fidget, snatching the wriggling creature from her death-grip as he passed.

Victoria pumped a fist in the air. "We're killing it! Let's see Team A beat that!"

Audrey rolled her eyes and laughed. "Victoria, *you're* on Team A!"

Victoria stared, too caught up in the moment to remember that she and Audrey had agreed to face off. Since Audrey and Victoria were hiding, no one could know where they were. They had trusted a few with an approximate location, however, which included those on their Berserk team. They had split the ten-person Plits team in half.

"Oh, right. Shit," she muttered, scanning the ground for another hundred-pointer. "I'm used to you and me being on the same team."

Audrey laughed. "It's all in good fun. There's another green one over there." Audrey nodded to the far wall and winked as a green fidget scampered by.

"You're the best!"

"I know!" Audrey jogged toward a golden fidget running around the fire-lit tunnel.

The Berserk game only lasted an hour before the scrapes, bruises, and broken bones tapped everyone out. Playing in the rocky tunnel had resulted in more wounds than a plush grassy playing field, and thus the blood and broken bones added up more quickly. Several elves limped with broken bones and bloody faces toward Fyrn, their chosen medic wizard. Audrey waited her turn, and Victoria kept her company as they neared the head of the line.

Fyrn, ever the grumpy old fart, groaned and cursed beneath his breath with every wound he healed.

"Oh, it's not that bad," Victoria chided him as his hand hovered over Audrey's broken pointer finger.

The digit snapped back into place, and Audrey sighed deeply. "Oh, thank goodness. That hurt like a bitch."

Fyrn grumbled, "I'm the most powerful wizard in Fairhaven, and I'm playing medic. It's disgraceful. Why couldn't you have summoned Diesel? Good gracious! I said relax, not order me around like I'm your intern."

"Summon Diesel? Yeah, great idea." Audrey patted Victoria on the back. "Your lover would certainly have dropped everything to be here. He might have just fawned over you rather than healing anyone, but at least it would have been hilarious."

"Hush, you," Victoria said, narrowing her eyes. She preferred Fyrn's grumbling to Diesel's incessant romantic advances any day.

Victoria was pretty sure she had a fractured arm and a dislocated shoulder, since the pain radiating from her left side was almost too much to bear. But her Rhazdon Artifact's healing ability would take care of her wounds, so she hadn't held up the line for others.

She sucked in shallow breaths while she waited for the magic to work its wonders, and she felt her shoulder sliding into place. With a final pop, it seated. Stretching her arms, Victoria sucked in a deep and happy breath. She shook them out, relishing the relief her mended joints gave her. "Thank you for agreeing to help us, Fyrn."

"Well, someone had to. Can't have an official medic come down to moderate your match, now can I? What if they're on Luak's payroll? What if…"

"Let's let him fume. Come on," Audrey whispered in Victoria's ear. She led the way back to their hideout while Fyrn bickered with Edgar about something to do with spoiled fruit. It didn't seem to matter to Fyrn what was he going on about, so long as he got to complain.

As they walked down the tunnel, the conversation from their makeshift Berserk field began to fade until it was nothing more than a hollow echo. The golden barrier Fyrn had set up to protect their match became visible around a corner, and they walked through it. A shiver went down Victoria's spine, and she looked over her shoulder. Fyrn had told her that from outside no one would even know it was there, which she now knew was true. That had kept the match safe and suspicious passersby out of the know.

She and Audrey strolled in silence for several minutes, Victoria enjoying the quiet.

But most of all, she enjoyed being with Audrey. She was relaxed again, and normal—like she used to be back when they didn't know about magic or Fairhaven. The tension from before their trip to Atlantis was gone, and they were once more simply friends.

They had been through hell *and* high water and there would be more disaster to come, but at least they had each other.

"I'm grateful you're my friend, Audrey." Victoria wrapped her arm around the Atlantean, its sudden weight disrupting Audrey's smooth gait a bit.

Audrey wrinkled her nose in mock disgust and poked Victoria's side. "Ew! When did you get all gooey and sentimental?"

"Hey, I gave you a fidget in today's match. You have to be nice to me." Victoria nudged Audrey's shoulder, grinning.

Audrey laughed. "In all seriousness, I'm grateful for you too, V. If you're beside me when all this goes south, I know we'll be okay."

"Likewise."

To the end, Victoria thought to herself. At this point they didn't even need to say it. Through pain, death, and murder, they would have each other's' backs.

CHAPTER SEVEN

Deep in a massive cave beneath Fairhaven, Audrey let out a long, slow breath as she focused her energy on the tiara fused to her forehead. Warmth swept through her body as she tapped into its powerful magic.

The crackle of flames filled her ears, and she could sense the heat from the dozens of magically-suspended flames Fyrn had littered through the cave for light. To concentrate, she did her best to tune out the soft trickle of the underground waterfall in the cave where she had been invited to train with Victoria and Fyrn.

A flicker of glee interrupted her thoughts. She couldn't help but inflate with pride at the thought of being invited to train with them. Fyrn had finally accepted Audrey as his pupil, and she felt at home practicing her gifts alongside her best friend. This meant she would only get better magically. She had already become an adept sword fighter, having taken on a snarx before she knew anything about Atlantis or her innate abilities. And now she would master her new magic as well.

Fucking *awesome.*

"Focus, damn it!" Fyrn shouted.

Audrey chuckled. She even enjoyed the grumpy old wizard's abuse. His yelling at her meant she was growing. Learning. It meant she was part of a brutal and unstoppable team.

You can do this, little one. The koi's melodic voice echoed in Audrey's mind.

Audrey's task was to use her Atlantean Artifact to shapeshift into a witch. Her grip tightened around the wand Fyrn had given her, a training tool used for witch kindergarteners to hone their skills. The dull rune-covered wood weighed on her palm, and she hoped she could make it spark to life.

She had never done this before—never even tried—but the thought of tapping into new power exhilarated her. Shifting into the form of a different race would give her that race's gifts and abilities. Even if she wouldn't have immediate mastery of them all, she could at least practice.

And wow, to be a witch for even a second was a dream that made her inner child beam with joy.

Fyrn tapped his staff on the rocky floor—probably to get her attention, since she had obviously messed up in her focus. His voice carried effortlessly through the cave. "This is tricky, Audrey. Clear your head. Think of nothing. Say nothing. Focus only on the wand and the shift. Don't be disappointed if you can't get it the first time."

Watch me, she thought with a smirk.

"She'll get it. Just watch," Victoria said from somewhere nearby, echoing Audrey's thought. Even with her eyes closed, Audrey smiled with gratitude.

Changing into a witch would be tough, because physically they didn't appear much different from humans. For this shift she had to change her body internally and alter how it interacted with magic, rather than just create a different appearance.

If the wand sparked to life, she would know she had succeeded.

It's an essence. A flow. A heartbeat, the koi said in Audrey's mind.

The thought simmered in her brain, and Audrey ran with it. The dull pulse of something distinctly *other* began to radiate through her fingertips, and for a second she panicked. The sensation reminded her momentarily of the voice that had all but taken over her back in Atlantis, urging her to stay and obey the king.

You are safe, the koi said in her mind.

With a deep, shaky breath, Audrey pushed the memories of her time as a brainwashed almost-princess from her mind.

She tried again to access the dull pulse from before, focusing her attention on the enchanted tiara resting on her brow. The sensation of *other* returned, and this time she let it be. Waited. Listened. Did her best not to judge.

After a few seconds, the magical heartbeat swelled into something immense. It thrummed against her very soul, brimming with power and promise.

The wand began to shake ever so slightly in her palm, twitching to the otherworldly pulse within her. Her breathing steady now, she waited.

In a sudden and almost violent rush, the dull wood

51

became something more. Something powerful. It called to her, urging her to tap into this new gift.

A bolt of energy burst from the tip, scorching the opposite wall. Stunned, Audrey gasped and took a step back, her grip on the rune-covered wand loosening.

When her focus shattered, the pulse faded until the wand was again nothing more than a dull stick of carved wood. As the rush of magic left her, exhaustion took its place. She felt suddenly heavy, as though she were wearing a wet coat.

But it didn't matter how tired she was—she had done it. For a split second, she had shifted and accessed another race's magical abilities. She smiled despite her sudden fatigue.

"Holy shit! *Yes!*" Victoria pumped her fist into the air and jumped, apparently too excited to contain herself.

To her credit, Audrey would have done the same had she not been so stunned by the experience. A witch's relationship with magic was beautiful. Otherworldly. Entrancing.

She had loved every second of it.

You will do great things, the koi said in Audrey's mind.

Audrey smiled, her grip tightening on the wand. "Damn right."

"I'm truly impressed," Fyrn said, leaning on his staff. "Have you tried this before?"

Audrey shook her head. "The koi helped me."

"Ah, the water spirit tied to your Artifact." Fyrn stroked his beard, eyes glazing as he stared at a nearby cave wall. "I do wish you had managed to secure a few of them for me. It disappoints me that there weren't any on the Atlanteans who crossed the portal into Fairhaven with you."

"Well, tough cookies, because we're never going back." Victoria crossed her arms and frowned. "Those assholes tried to kill me and Diesel."

Audrey wistfully looked at the waterfall. A part of her soul called for her to return. Atlantis was full of jackasses, sure, but it was her home. The Atlantean within her ached to go back, but she suppressed the nostalgic desire with a sharp breath and a grimace.

The Atlanteans had tried to take Victoria from her—Audrey's *true* family—and not even a homeland and a kingdom were worth risking her friend's life. "I definitely think we should stay away. Besides, after killing their General and defying their king we would hardly be welcome."

Fyrn paced the small cave in which they were training. "True. Regardless, I believe much of your connection to your Artifact comes from your heritage, Audrey. Should Victoria or I try to connect with one, we would likely have far more trouble mastering its gifts. I doubt we would have pleasant experiences with the spirits tied to the Atlantean Artifacts, either."

Audrey shrugged. It was probably true, but she wasn't proud of the elitist nature of her newly-discovered people.

Fyrn sighed. "Ah, well. We have other means of helping Victoria achieve the strength she requires. Back to work, both of you. Audrey, we have a few more forms to try."

The mood shifted suddenly, and neither spoke or moved despite Fyrn's command. Victoria bit her nail, eyes out of focus as she stared at the cave wall. Audrey knew that look—Victoria was trying to hide her nerves about the dark magic in her future.

Audrey set her hand on Victoria's shoulder. "You'll be okay, V. Another Rhazdon Artifact isn't going to change who you are. It'll just make you more badass."

Victoria looked at her and, after flashing a bittersweet expression containing simultaneous panic and gratitude, smiled. "I know. Especially when I have you to keep me in check and Fyrn to shout obscenities."

"Damn it all, will you two focus?" Fyrn scowled.

"See?" Victoria chuckled.

Fyrn pointed at Audrey. "We don't have enough time to train you fully in the ways of magical combat, but Bertha has done a fine job of preparing you in swordplay. For now, therefore, we need to make sure you can handle a few more forms before we leave tomorrow. Now, Audrey, an ogre, if you please."

Audrey nodded and took a deep breath. This one she had done successfully twice, and she knew she could do it again.

Exhaustion pulled on her limbs and urged her to rest, but she couldn't. Not now. They had dark magic to find, and Audrey had to be at the top of her game if she was going to keep Victoria out of harm's way.

CHAPTER EIGHT

Victoria was packing her bags. They would leave in an hour.

She couldn't help the excited tremble in her hands as she stuffed her clothes unceremoniously into her pack. Screw folding her shirts! Her mind wandered over what awaited them in the rocky desert of Arizona, where her new Rhazdon Artifact had been hidden for centuries.

And soon it would be hers. Soon she would have six terrifying abilities instead of just three.

She paused, tensing at the thought of more dark magic in her blood. Fyrn had said there might even be more Rhazdon Artifacts down the line. More blood. More death.

She sucked a deep breath through her teeth. Victoria needed to focus her mind on something—*anything*—else.

Their trip to Sedona would be successful. If she focused only on the next step, she wouldn't panic about what would come after.

Sedona was a magical marvel that even the humans

MARTHA CARR & MICHAEL ANDERLE

knew was special. Fyrn had told her a bit of the lore, but only enough to whet her appetite. There had once been a kemana there deep beneath the ground, but someone had destroyed it thousands of years ago. Someone powerful. Someone deadly. According to rumor, there had only been one survivor.

A witch. And once she had left, she had never gone back.

Rumor was, something had taken over the ruins. Something dark. Whoever—or whatever—now lurked there would take no prisoners, and yet she and the people she cared most about in this world were about to kick in the front door.

What could go wrong?

"Victoria my love, you look as ravishing as ever," a familiar voice said from her doorway.

She rubbed her face and didn't bother to stifle her groan. "Don't you have a city council to run, Diesel?"

"I do, but I had to see my lady off. I will miss you, dearest."

Goddamn it. She ignored him and continued to stuff her clothes into her pack without noticing what she was putting in.

Behind her, he snapped his fingers. The clothes that were still piled on her bed folded instantaneously and leapt into her bag, while the clothes and other things within folded themselves or tucked themselves into the various pockets. In seconds, her packing had been done for her.

Even the underwear.

She shot him a glare at the thought of his touching—

even magically—her personal effects, and he flashed the charming smile that would have dropped most women's pants. Victoria, however, merely rolled her eyes. "Thanks."

"Anything for you."

Victoria was about to tell him—again—that she wasn't interested, but a wayward thought crossed her mind. She cast a glance over her shoulder at the wizard who had gained the king's trust. "Is King Bornt still alive?"

Diesel's smile faltered, and he leaned against the door-frame. "No one has seen him in three weeks. He sends orders from his locked room, but will allow no one to enter. I suspect he's long dead, and that the orders are coming from Luak himself. Luak is slowly taking over the council, buying the loyalty of one member after another. I don't think we have much time before he takes over completely."

"Fabulous." Victoria rubbed her temples, frustrated. Her enemy would soon have access to Fairhaven's treasury and Army to hunt her down, as if things weren't already bad enough.

Diesel rubbed his jaw. "Speaking of which, you have become Public Enemy Number One, Victoria. There's a hundred-thousand-denni reward for anyone who brings you to the throne room alive, and a death sentence for anyone who kills you."

Victoria tensed, grateful Diesel was on her side even if he was annoying as hell sometimes. "Where do they think I am?"

"In the tunnels below the city."

She frowned. It wasn't far from the truth, and the

memory of the tingle of eyes on her back sent a shiver down her spine. Something had followed her through the tunnels about half the times she had gone down there. Though she had lost it several times, there was always the chance whoever it was knew where she had been hiding, or at least the general area.

But why hadn't this person attacked?

"Something has been following me in the tunnels," she confessed, fussing with the snaps and pockets on her pack to distract herself.

"Oh, that was one of my spies. I wanted to ensure you're safe. You're quite good at losing him, though."

Victoria smacked Diesel's shoulder. "What the hell?"

He lifted his hands in surrender. "I needed to know you were okay, my love. I worry, you know? You never write, you never visit me…"

She ran a hand through her hair and threw the pack over her shoulder, glaring at him but simultaneously grateful the mystery had been solved. "At least it's not Luak. I was wondering why I hadn't been attacked."

"I wouldn't have allowed it."

She shook her head, but couldn't suppress the chuckle. *This damn wizard is unrelenting.*

Her smile fell, however, when she thought again of the probably-dead king. This had to stop.

Victoria tightened the strap on her shoulder. "Keep a lookout while we're gone. Luak won't trust anyone with specifics of his plans, but gather whatever you can."

Fyrn's heavy footsteps thudded as he climbed the stairs. "He's coming with us," the old wizard said absently as he passed the door. In seconds he was gone, as though he hadn't pulled the rug out from under her with a simple statement.

Diesel grinned. Victoria did not.

"Are you joking?" she shouted.

Fyrn's voice thundered through the corridor from somewhere down the hall. "We need all the help we can get, Victoria. I don't like it either."

Diesel took a final step into the room, his frame as tall as the doorway as he leaned against the wall and casually slipped his hands into his pockets. Any other woman would have swooned at the imposing man standing in her bedroom, but Victoria knew him better than most.

His smile widened. "I see you can't bear to be away from me, darling Victoria. Secretly asking your mentor to allow me to come while protesting the decision in order to preserve your fierce public persona? It's endearing."

"Don't you pack yet." She pointed a finger at the handsome wizard and pushed past him, crossing the hallway to give her mentor a piece of her mind.

The door at the end of the hall stood open, and she leaned against the frame. "Fyrn, a word."

"Not now, Victoria. Finish packing." The old wizard pulled more vials filled with glowing green liquid off the shelves.

"Wait, what are those?" She pointed to the various bottles.

"I brewed healing tonics and a few explosives to be on the safe side. I figured it would be best that you have a small armory should an invasion take place."

"And you were going to tell me about this when?"

He shrugged. "I was getting to it."

Victoria rolled her eyes, but figured she should choose her battles wisely. "Diesel can't come."

Fyrn, to his credit, smirked and lifted one scraggly eyebrow. "*You* are giving *me* orders now?"

Exasperated, she pointed through the wall in the general direction of the celebrity wizard in her bedroom. "Yeah, if it's about him joining us on yet another long and grueling journey, Fyrn. *He's not coming.*"

"We need him."

She sighed, already having a hunch what this was really about. "He helped us escape Atlantis. I appreciate everything he did. I doubt we could have escaped without him, but—"

"I believe you could have escaped without him, but as I expected, he was an asset. He may have saved your life, Victoria."

She sighed, hands in her pockets as she stared at the floor. She hated to admit she owed Diesel anything, but he had become part of the group. He had dropped everything to come with them once, and she was sure he would do it again. "Yeah, but—"

"But you're sick of his advances," Fyrn finished.

Victoria nodded. "It's exhausting and distracting."

Fyrn shrugged. "Get over it."

"What?"

"Get over it," Fyrn repeated, as though she hadn't heard him.

She gritted her teeth. "Fyrn, when a woman says, 'What,' it's not that she didn't hear you. She's giving you a chance to change your answer."

He huffed. "Diesel is a powerful asset, and loyal to you. He would never dream of hurting you, and he would follow you to hell if you asked him to. If it were me, I would consider it a small price to pay and gladly accept him on my team."

She grimaced a bit at the image of Diesel fawning over her grumpy old mentor, and quickly pushed the thought away. "Well sure, but he's not inches away from pinching your ass at any moment."

Fyrn sighed. "Victoria, we need to get out of the city soon. One of my spies just visited and said Luak's plans have changed. I'm not sure what happened, but that psychotic elf is moving everything forward. All the murders. All the raids. *Everything.* Perhaps he has a general idea where you are. If so, he'll begin burning houses to flush you out."

Victoria's jaw snapped shut with an audible click. She couldn't speak for several moments, and when she did it came out as a harsh whisper. "Shit."

Fyrn nodded. "To make matters worse, there are rumors of assassinations and missing political figures in the castle. Important senators and generals have disappeared, some as recently as thirty minutes ago, according to my spies. If Diesel hadn't been here checking on you he would have already been detained, or possibly killed. He's powerful, but not even *he* can take on a whole army by himself. The bloodshed in the castle right now is unheard of. His affection for you saved his life."

Victoria's body went cold, and she could feel the color draining from her face. Diesel was one of her own, even with his annoying personality. She cared about the wizard, and wanted him on her team. The close call sent a shiver through her body.

But after the chill came the rage. She had almost lost yet another person she cared about to that power-hungry Light Elf. Her panic quickly faded into hatred. Anger. Bloodlust.

She would fucking *destroy* Luak, and he would be in utter agony every second of his death. She would see to that.

Fyrn paused in his packing and scanned her face. "Now that you fully understand the threat, can Diesel come?"

She nodded. *Damn it.* "I'm glad he isn't dead."

"As am I," Fyrn said softly, a look of sadness on his face as he shoved yet another green vial into his seemingly bottomless bag.

"But I'm going to set boundaries," Victoria warned.

Fyrn nodded. "Good. We don't have any time to lose."

Victoria walked into the hallway, mind still stuck in the realization that she had almost lost one of her friends. If Diesel hadn't left the castle to see her off, he would be dead.

She couldn't quite wrap her head around it.

"Is everything all right, Victoria?" Diesel asked, his pestering charm dropping for a moment into true concern as she stepped into the hallway.

Victoria eyed him for a moment, then hugged him. Her arms wrapped around his solid midsection, and she pulled him close without saying a word.

Apparently baffled, he hesitated briefly before wrapping his arms around her.

"Don't die, you big idiot," she said softly. With that, she

trotted down the stairs, leaving a thoroughly confused wizard in her wake.

They had to get the hell out of here. The sooner they got this new Rhazdon Artifact, the sooner she could stop Luak's tyranny.

CHAPTER NINE

After the purely platonic hug, Diesel didn't seem to understand Victoria's concept of boundaries.

Ugh.

When they boarded the plane to Sedona, their appearances changed by the glamours Fyrn had put together for them, Victoria took one of the four first-class seats she had bought with her parents' insurance money.

If they were going to fly, they were going to do it in style.

Across the aisle, Fyrn sported a crisp black business suit. Though he wore his wizard robes in reality, the glamour affected everything from his shoes to his hairstyle. He had short hair, which honestly suited him far better than the scraggly-wizard look. Two flight attendants had already stopped by to offer him liquor and fruit no one else was getting, and Victoria couldn't help but roll her eyes at their obvious flirting.

They had agreed on their story on the way over. Fyrn was playing the part of a rich tycoon of some sort, which was easy for him since he was used to bossing people around. Victoria and Audrey had been glamoured to be his raven-haired daughters and wore sleek black dresses, because apparently black was Fyrn's favorite glamour-color.

At Victoria's request, Diesel had been dressed to look like their butler.

Styx was hidden in a luxurious and charmed carry-on bag in the bins above their seats, no doubt devouring the oranges she had left in there for him. She eyed the overhead compartment, wondering if she should make sure he had enough air, but Fyrn had assured her at least two dozen times that her pet pixie would be safe in the bag.

Much to her surprise, Fyrn had also put his and Diesel's staffs in the upper compartment, having charmed them both to look like very long poster tubes.

Diesel had finagled himself into the seat beside Victoria, and now rested his arm over her shoulders. Though she continually reminded him it was improper for the butler to hit on his boss's daughter, he didn't seem to care about keeping their cover story alive.

His arm had been resting behind her head for at least an hour, but it was easier to roll her eyes than push him away.

If it were anyone else being this persistent, Victoria would have kicked him in the chest or slapped some sense into him. But this was Diesel. He was harmless. Annoying, yes. But harmless.

Something shifted in Victoria's peripheral vision and she lifted her head to see Audrey waving to get her attention. Victoria raised one eyebrow to communicate. *What?*

Audrey nodded at Diesel and made a kissing motion with her lips.

Victoria flipped her best friend off, and Audrey just laughed.

Back in the airport, Audrey had called her parents while they waited for their flight. Victoria's chest had tightened at the reminder of what she no longer had, but she had forced herself to listen anyway. It was neat to hear the way Audrey's voice shifted when she spoke with her parents. She always sounded so happy. Audrey had made it sound like they were jet-setting off to yet another foreign country, keeping the lie of their backpacking trip through Europe alive and well.

Victoria still didn't like lying to Mr. and Mrs. Xavier, but it was better than telling them the truth. At least Audrey *was* keeping in touch with her parents. The fact warmed Victoria's heart, even if that organ panged with her own loss at the same time.

As the plane rumbled beneath her, Victoria surveyed the first-class cabin. Most of the travelers conversed in hushed tones, no doubt networking or trying to rub elbows with someone important. A few wore headphones and nodded silently to themselves, eyes closed as they listened to whatever piped through their speakers. One little girl in the back kicked her feet at the seat in front of her, her short legs missing the chair by inches.

A thin curtain separated the first-class cabin from coach seating, and Victoria couldn't help but think it was weird to be up front. On the rare occasions she had flown in her life—tickets were expensive, after all, and she had always been poor—she and her parents had always traveled in cattle class.

Being rich was weird. Awesome, but weird.

Being back in the human world after living in Fairhaven for so long was also surreal. To see her fellow humans munching on apple slices and perusing the complimentary tablets for a movie to watch reminded her of her life before magic. Before Fairhaven. Before Luak. Before—

Before her parents were killed.

Gritting her teeth, she settled into her chair and did her best not to seethe with hatred. Her grip on the padded armrest tightened, and she glared at the seat in front of her.

"Are you all right, my dear?" Diesel asked, setting one hand on hers.

She shook him off. "Boundaries, man. *Boundaries.*"

He lifted his hands in defeat. "I apologize, but my question still stands. Don't make me get out my truth dagger."

The chair in front of Victoria shifted and a man peeked over the headrest, quizzically glancing at Diesel.

Victoria grinned. Out of context, it must have sounded like Diesel had used an innuendo. To let off some steam, she winked at the man in front of her who was butting into their conversation. "Do you want to see his *truth dagger* for yourself?"

He blushed and settled back into his seat, clearing his throat a few times too many for it to be natural. Victoria stifled her laughter and added below her breath, "It's *my* truth dagger, remember?"

Diesel grinned. "Of course, my love, but couples share."

With a groan and a chuckle, she leaned against the

cushy headrest and tried to relax. It was only a two hour flight, so she could suffer through his advances a little while longer. Their journey, however, would be a long one. She might as well enjoy first class while she was here.

On a dusty desert road near Sedona, Victoria panicked and grabbed the handle above the window of their rented four-door sedan. Rocks protruded from the road like icebergs waiting to carve open something important in the bottom of the car, and she didn't like this one bit.

Styx clung to her hair, hiding in her locks in case anyone passed them on the empty road. So far they had only seen one dusty red pickup as it sped by, the driver laughing and shaking his head as he surveyed the tiny four-door sedan.

They had left the highway several miles ago, and it seemed as though they were in way over their heads. Their car that would be torn open by the rocky road at any minute.

Diesel drove as fast as he safely could while dodging the biggest obstacles, grumbling to himself about being able to flatten the road magically if only the Order of the Silver Griffins would let him perform magic on Earth. Even when it seemed like no one was watching, someone probably was. He couldn't risk it, and thus they followed the bouncy road and cringed with every scrape of rock against the car's metal underbelly.

"Why didn't we just use a portal?" Audrey asked from

the backseat, her arms pressed against the windowsill and middle seat to keep her balance in the chaotic car.

Fyrn huffed. "Portals are dangerous, and in most cases illegal. Mundane travel is safer. There's less chance of you getting lost in the in-between. Would you rather live for eternity as a ghost lost between worlds?"

Audrey grumbled and stared out the window as the car hit another rock-berg. She winced. "Maybe."

Victoria chuckled to herself as Diesel drove them around a particularly large boulder. "I can't believe this is the best route."

"I'm following the little magic man, okay?" Diesel snapped, uncharacteristically tense.

For a moment Victoria felt bad for pushing his buttons, but then her brain caught up with what he had said. "'The little magic man?'"

Diesel gestured to the GPS he had rented with the car. The arrow representing their sedan blinked along a blue route, and the estimated arrival time kept creeping backward as they drove under the unpaved road's ludicrously high speed limit.

"If you don't know what a GPS is, I'm astonished you know how to drive," Victoria said.

Diesel shrugged, his obnoxious charm creeping back into his face for a second. "There's much you don't know about me, my love. I can pull over if you'd like to explore the subject for an hour or two."

Ah, there's the old Diesel. Victoria rolled her eyes.

As the minutes passed, the blinking blue arrow grew closer to the orange pin that represented their destination. Eager to be out of the jostling car, Victoria sat on the edge of her seat and peered into the horizon. Heat simmered along the dusty road, and in the distance Victoria thought she could make out something dark gray blocking their path. "What's that?"

Everyone in the car peered forward, eyes squinting as they studied the object. Heat waves continued to obscure most of it. It wasn't until they got nearer that they could make out the smooth gleam of asphalt and a sign pointing them to the interstate.

A road. And not just any road—a perfectly smooth road leading from the highway. All along, there had been a much smoother route to take.

In unison, Victoria, Fyrn, and Audrey turned their heads to glare at Diesel for the last hour of torture. He tensed his jaw, but refused to meet their gazes.

"Idiot boy," Fyrn muttered under his breath.

Once on the asphalt, their little car sputtered as if with gratitude and they turned left, racing toward the destination on the GPS. In a matter of minutes, Diesel parked in an empty lot. Everyone stepped out of the car, stretching and mumbling about the ride as they tried to shake away the soreness.

"*I'm* driving on the way back," Victoria said, snatching the keys from Diesel's hand. This time *he* rolled his eyes. Victoria smirked. She seemed to be rubbing off on both the wizards in her life.

Arms crossed, Audrey looked around. "Where are we, Fyrn?"

Victoria stared across the empty parking lot at a guard house which sat beside a concrete walkway that cut through the desert underbrush. A metal awning stretched over a picnic table, providing shade and a place for tourists to whip out their picnic baskets. Beige sand covered much of the desert around them, though there were an abundance of short bushes with twisted trunks that cast limited shade from the harsh sun.

Above them stretched a massive hill, so high Victoria couldn't tell what lay at its peak. The concrete path by the guard station wound toward the peak, dotted with stairs and occasionally decorated with handrails on the steeper parts.

Fyrn set his hands on his hips and stared at the hill. "Montezuma's Well."

Victoria quirked an eyebrow. "That sounds ominous."

Fyrn nodded. "It's supposed to. This is a spring, one filled with leeches and monsters the likes of which you can't even imagine."

Victoria stared at the unassuming hill and whistled. "There's a spring up there?"

"It's more of a massive sinkhole, but yes. It's technically a spring."

Audrey shielded her eyes with her hands. "We're not going for a swim, are we?"

"No," Diesel answered.

Thank goodness. Victoria had enough of watery monsters back in Atlantis. She glanced toward Audrey, who caught her eye and nodded. They had apparently had the same thought.

His staff tapping along the pavement, Fyrn led the way up the path and huffed a bit with the effort of the steep climb. "Sedona is a vast and powerful place rife with magic. Even the humans know that. This isn't an accident, of course. There was once a kemana below the ground, much like Fairhaven is built within the rock. The Sedona kemana was a place for witches and wizards, a haven for the most powerful of our kind. The massive city sprawled for miles in every direction. In those days we had formidable numbers, and most lived here."

Diesel nodded and offered Victoria a hand, which she ignored. He didn't seem fazed. "The old lore says a flood destroyed them, but we all know better. Kemanas are protected by powerful magic, the kind that would never allow a natural disaster to have any effect. No, the flood was a result of something greater. Something attacked the kemana and destroyed it, and it's been leaking magic ever since. Only one girl escaped the carnage, and she joined a local human tribe aboveground."

"Do you think it's true? Or is that just a legend?" Victoria asked.

Diesel shrugged. "It's hard to tell. If it is true, she left her magical heritage in the past and refused to ever write or speak of what happened."

"But I think I know," Fyrn said ominously.

"Care to share with the class?" Victoria asked, puffing as she trotted up several steep steps.

Fyrn leaned on his staff as they neared the top of the hill. "They were sabotaged from within. Someone betrayed them."

Victoria frowned, her mind racing with possibilities of what really happened all those centuries ago.

Fyrn continued, "These were powerful witches and wizards, who would not be taken down by some beast. Many modern members of the Order of the Silver Griffin claim to have bloodlines from this kemana as a point of pride, whether or not it's true."

"I have the bloodline, for instance," Diesel said with a grin.

Fyrn shook his head and ignored the comment. "For such powerful witches and wizards to lose their city, they must have been infiltrated. It's the only answer that makes sense. Someone either wanted something they had—"

"Or wanted to hide something so it would never be found," Victoria finished, her lips almost moving on their own. It all clicked into place for her in that moment, and Fyrn gave her a curt nod.

This long-lost magical city had been chosen for its power to hide something deadly. Something dangerous.

The Rhazdon Artifact she was here to find.

She tightened her fist, frowning a bit at the severity of the situation.

The party reached the top, and the stunning vista stole Victoria's breath. For a moment she could only stand still and mutter a soft, "Wow."

Fyrn took a deep breath. "Welcome to Montezuma's Well, entrance to the once-great kemana of Lochrose."

Victoria's eyes scanned the impressive scene, not entirely sure where to look first. A massive pool of water lay below them, with only a thin metal rail between solid ground and a fifty-foot fall into the murky depths. Mountains rose into the sky beyond the water-filled sinkhole, and a dusting of short trees with twisted trunks covered the landscape along the rim.

Most impressively, the ruins of a once-great dwelling

were built into the rock wall to their left, with the basic structure still standing. A window and doorway were visible in the remnants of the building, but not much else was left.

Audrey pointed to the ancient home. "That's not where we're going, is it?"

Diesel shook his head. "That's an ancient native ruin, one we will respect and avoid. It's best not to touch the remains of other cultures. What we seek is underground."

"Here," Fyrn said, hardly looking at the scenery.

Victoria pried her eyes away from the beautiful spring as he began to descend along the cliff wall. "What are you doing?"

"Walking down the stairs," he said without looking back. She tiptoed closer to the edge, and sure enough—smooth, steep steps that led to the water had been carved into the cliff wall.

"I thought you said we weren't going for a swim," Audrey said dryly.

"Will you three hurry up?" Fyrn snapped, not answering Audrey's concern.

Frowning, Victoria followed her mentor down the stairs, with Audrey and Diesel hot on her heels. The steps were easy enough to hurry down and open to the public, which suggested they had been added by the park rangers. It was a neat effect, walking into the sinkhole—like descending into something ancient and forbidden. Victoria couldn't help the childish grin that snuck onto her face as they neared the rocky shore.

Victoria trailed her fingertips along the cliff as they descended, still mesmerized by the magical place. It radiated life and energy, and called to her with a siren song she didn't fully understand. "Where are we going?"

"The entrance to the long-lost city," Fyrn said absently from the bottom of the steps. He meandered along the shoreline, weaving between boulders and the occasional scraggly tree as though searching for something. He tapped his staff on the ground with every step, the dull *thunk* like a drunk and tired woodpecker stabbing a tree without rhythm or consistency.

"But what are you—"

The staff struck a dent in the rocky ground, and a sharp vibration filled the air. It hummed through the sinkhole like a choir in a cathedral, so loud that Victoria held her ears. She and Audrey cringed, almost kneeling under the intensity of the sound.

Fyrn and Diesel, however, seemed utterly unaffected. Fyrn muttered something under his breath, and a flash of light erupted from the tip of his staff. The overpowering ringing faded.

Diesel helped Victoria to her feet. "Are you all right?"

Victoria nodded. "What the hell was that?"

Fyrn grumbled under his breath. "A defense mechanism to ward off non-wizards. I should have expected it, but I didn't think it would still be active after all these years. Apologies, girls."

Audrey rubbed her temples and muttered something about where he could shove his apologies. Victoria smacked her friend's shoulder, and the Atlantean shrugged unashamedly.

His staff still rooted in the small indent, Fyrn set his hand against the jagged wall nearby. Instead of his palm pressing on the rock, however, his hand disappeared into the cliff. He nodded to himself and gestured to the wall. "In you go."

"But it's... Where's the door? All I see is you missing a hand," Audrey said.

"Come on, come on," Fyrn said, waving them through as he eyed the top of the stairs.

Victoria followed his gaze, and a light bulb went off in her head. The shrill vibration would no doubt draw the attention of anyone nearby, and while they hadn't seen anyone, it didn't mean their small party was in the clear.

Victoria went first, summoning her sword in case they encountered anything deadly on the other side. Braced for battle, she charged through the gap.

The rock rippled as she passed, and she sucked in a breath as her body trembled with the sensation.

Styx, apparently picking up on her frenzied energy, sailed out of his hiding place in her hair and lifted his tiny hands as though he would karate-chop the first thing he saw into submission.

Victoria skidded to a halt on the other side with her magical blade in her hand and surveyed her surroundings. She was in a silent pitch-black cave. Not even the whisper of a draft or the drop of water on the ground broke the quiet.

She held her breath, body tensed for an attack.

Feet shuffled behind her, and with a burst of light Audrey and Diesel entered. Fyrn jumped in behind them, and their forms vanished into the darkness when the light from outside was cut off.

Audrey's voice echoed through the dark cave, making

Victoria jump. "If it's just a hidden door, can't humans stumble in accidentally?"

"A wizard must be present for it to open," Diesel said with a shrug.

"Elitists," Audrey said with a chuckle.

Victoria laughed, the tension of the moment broken by her friend's hypocrisy.

"Ladies, focus," Fyrn said.

The familiar tap of Fyrn's staff on hard ground echoed through the space. The crystal in the top of his staff shimmered to life, casting a dim glow on his weathered face. Within seconds, bands of light radiated from the stone like ripples on a pond.

The bands passed through Victoria, tickling a little, and hit the wall. The wall seemed to shiver as it absorbed his magic, the movement like a dog shaking off water. Victoria tensed for battle, unnerved by the almost human movement of the walls around her.

Fyrn, however, looked as bored as if he were surveying a rainy sky.

Humming filled the cave once more, and the walls began to sparkle. One by one, gemstones appeared and glimmered like stars in a night sky. Purple, blue, green, pink—the wall erupted into a rainbow of color. Brilliant light radiated from the crystals around them, eliciting a few stunned gasps.

Fast as lightning, the colorful illumination spread down a tunnel that had been shrouded in darkness.

What had been an impossibly dark cave now glowed with light radiating from the brilliant crystals embedded in the cave wall. Styx muttered his usual gibberish, shoulders slumping as he stared around. Even Victoria relaxed, marveling at the sight. "It's beautiful."

Fyrn huffed. "Much of Lochrose is beautiful, designed to capture your attention while something else kills you. Let's go. Whatever is down here already knows we're here. The warning signal out front would have alerted it, as will these crystals."

"Maybe we shouldn't have lit the crystals, then," Victoria said, hands on her hips.

He eyed her warily. "These tunnels are designed to confuse. To mislead. To kill. Without the light, we would be lost in their depths forever."

A thought occurred to Victoria. Not long ago, Fyrn had trusted her with the knowledge of a powerful weapon he was building. A secret, one he had told only her and Audrey. He had cursed the tunnels that led to that project cave in a similar way to the Lochrose tunnels, and she wondered how much of his magical protection had been inspired by the once-great city they were going to visit.

Fyrn was a mystery, one she would probably never fully unravel. Every time she thought she knew her mentor, he revealed something else.

If she hadn't already trusted him with her life, that fact might have unnerved her.

CHAPTER TEN

The tunnel went on forever, and Audrey didn't like it one bit. This place set her nerves on fire and made her want to bolt. Every fiber in her being screamed at her to escape and go somewhere else.

Victoria and Styx may have gaped at the glowing jewels embedded in the rock walls and ceiling, but Audrey kept one hand on her sword hilt. The powerful Atlantean crystals she had been given pressed against her palm, their energy sparking in her body even as she kept it at bay.

This place freaked her out, and she couldn't say why.

Maybe it was the sensation of going deep underground. Now and then her ears popped, even though the tunnel didn't seem to slope much, if at all. They walked for what felt like ages, yet her body wasn't tired. She had no sense of time, no concept of where they were or whether she should be hungry.

"Fyrn, how long have we been walking?" Audrey finally asked.

The old wizard sighed. "Time has no meaning down

here, Audrey. You and Victoria will never tire or get hungry. You will have no sense of what time it is or where we are until we get to Lochrose. It's another charm meant to disrupt and disorient those who shouldn't be here."

"You guys have a lot of those nasty little charms down here, huh?"

He nodded. "We're wizards. There's a reason you don't see many of our kind in big cities."

"We don't trust easily," Diesel elaborated, shoulders squared and an uncharacteristic frown on his face.

Shit! If even Diesel was uneasy, this was more serious than Audrey had originally thought. He hadn't tried to hit on Victoria once since they had entered the cave, and that meant he was alert for trouble.

Audrey huffed, grip tightening on her sword's hilt for comfort.

They went around a bend and the glowing crystals ended in a pool of blackness, as if the world simply stopped existing at the end of this tunnel. There was no light, no sense of distance, nothing. Only the dark.

Audrey tensed. "Watch out."

"It's a cave-in," Diesel said, patting Audrey's shoulder.

"You're certainly wound tight," Victoria said softly, eyeing Audrey with concern as Diesel quickened his pace to reach the cave-in first.

"This place freaks me out," Audrey said with a broad gesture to the walls around her.

"It reminds me of a slightly darker Atlantis, actually," Victoria said with a cheeky smile.

Audrey's frown deepened. "Our tunnels were pretty, and had life and water. This is just oppressive."

Victoria's smile faded a bit, the difference so subtle that it was barely noticeable in the rainbow of light streaming from the crystals around them. "There's beauty here too, Audrey. You were at home in Atlantis, even in the caves. Diesel and I were not. It's good to be alert, but you're going to stress yourself and maybe even burn out if you're this tense the entire time we're down here. Try to find a happy place between 'daydreaming' and 'about to blow a hole in the wall,' okay?"

Audrey nodded, but she didn't mean it. It was merely a hunch, but she figured only getting the hell out of this place would calm her nerves. The Lochrose tunnels just didn't sit right with her.

The witches and wizards never liked your kind, the koi said in her mind.

This caught Audrey's attention. "Wizards don't like Atlanteans?"

It used to be so. There are wards here just for you, Audrey. Spells your friends will not feel. Wars were fought in centuries past between your peoples. There were times when a wizard would kill an Atlantean without pausing to consider if the Atlantean deserved it. They were locked in a bloody struggle for eons.

Audrey glanced at Fyrn and Diesel, whose respective staffs were raised and glowing as they sifted through the rubble blocking the path. "Good thing times change, huh?"

Indeed, the koi answered.

"What?" Victoria asked from a few paces ahead.

"Nothing. Just muttering to myself," Audrey said.

Victoria eyed her suspiciously, but Audrey smiled. She didn't want to further complicate things. If the legends were true, then no wizards or witches still lived here anyway. These were old enchantments. Racist ones, sure, but old and forgotten.

Besides, she had two wizards on her side. What could happen?

Fyrn grumbled, "Audrey, if you could use your crystal to—"

The ground shook and pebbles began to fall from the ceiling, interrupting him. A hollow roar blasted through the cave like a ghost screaming through the veil between worlds. It came from everywhere and nowhere, through the rock and through the floor. It was all Audrey could do to stay on her feet as the mighty sound rattled her bones.

At the end of the hall, the darkness began to morph. Bit by bit, the rocks shifted and piled onto each other as if lifted by invisible hands. Diesel and Fyrn stepped back, staffs raised, and Audrey realized with a sudden rush of panic that neither of them were controlling this.

Not sure what else to do, Audrey drew her sword and charged it with the white energy of the crystal in the tight grip of her free hand. Victoria summoned the gleaming magical blade of her Rhazdon Artifact and aimed it toward the self-piling rocks. Together, they flanked the two wizards and prepared for whatever came next.

At least, Audrey *thought* she had been prepared.

The rocks formed the rough shape of a man twice their height, and thick arms hung at its side as more rocks formed a head. The boulders clung together seemingly by sheer will, and Audrey could see the light of the cave behind the creature through gaps in its biceps and thighs where tendon and bone should have been.

"What the fuck is that?" Victoria screamed.

Audrey nodded, shock and disbelief locking her mouth even though she wanted nothing more than to voice a similar sentiment.

"A golem! Get back!" Diesel shouted.

"Damn it all!" Fyrn aimed his staff at the creature and fired just as the head finished forming. Two red eyes popped open and glared at them.

The burst of light from Fyrn's staff burned a hole through the creature's forehead, but instead of falling to the ground dead as any normal being would, it merely screamed as though Fyrn had pissed it off.

"Fyrn, how do we kill it?" Victoria yelled.

The monster charged, and all four dodged out of the way. Audrey barely managed to roll out of reach as it grabbed for her. Its massive rocky fist sailed toward her head, and she ducked once more. It roared, the billowing sound shaking her to the bone, but she held her ground when it attacked again.

Victoria jumped between Audrey and the creature, which never took its eyes off Audrey. It seemed to watch her every step, every swing of her sword, every bend of her knees. It was as though only she and the golem were in the cave.

Great, an admirer, she thought.

It screamed again and charged for her. She ducked, rolling out of the way while its hand closed in the space where her head had been only a second prior. They needed a plan, but Audrey had no idea how to destroy this thing.

"Fyrn! Plan?" Victoria shouted.

"Remove its heart!" the old wizard replied, shooting

MARTHA CARR & MICHAEL ANDERLE

another beam toward the monster's chest. It burst through the rock, leaving a baseball-sized hole in the monster. A dim red glow radiated from within, made more prominent by the dark cave.

The golem swung a hulking fist at Audrey, but Victoria dove for the creature and took the brunt of the blow. She gritted her teeth, no doubt biting back the pain of absorbing such a strike, and Audrey couldn't help but be grateful for her friend's innate healing ability.

With every ounce of her strength, Victoria clung to the beast's arm. It threw her over its head, and she sailed into the air. Her hair hovered around her face, and she fell as though she were submerged in water. For a moment time seemed to stop.

Audrey couldn't tell at first what Victoria's plan was, but as gravity pulled her back to the ground she lifted her sword and swung at the monster's shoulder. The golem's arm was sheered clean off and shattered on the floor.

The creature screamed. Victoria landed on her feet just as the other arm sailed over her head then dropped, rolling until she was out of reach.

"Victoria, be careful!" Diesel shouted.

"Well, the goal is to not die, so *duh!*" she yelled back.

The golem returned its attention to Audrey and charged her like a one-armed gorilla, which would have been hilarious in almost any other circumstance.

Audrey spun out of the way and lifted her sword to take off the creature's other arm. Before she could, two brilliant bursts of light tore through the creature's torso.

Audrey spun on her heel to see the two wizards' faces

set in grim determination while they stared down the beast like a scraggly father and son duo.

Although riddled with holes—none of which were Audrey's doing—the golem never took its eyes from her. It reached for her with its remaining massive hand, which she was pretty sure would crush her face.

"Enough!" Audrey was done with this monster and its fixation on her. Pissed off and ready to kill, she tightened her grip on the crystal she still held. A bolt of brilliant white light burst from her hand, aimed for the red glow in the golem's chest.

As it hit, the white light of her Atlantean magic morphed and twisted into something else. The pure white brilliance bled into the dark red glow, and seconds later they heard the fragile crunch of shattering glass. The monster stilled as though it had run out of batteries. The red glow in its eyes faded, and the remaining rocks that had once comprised its body almost deafened them as they clattered to the ground in a heap.

Still on one knee with the other leg braced for balance, Audrey didn't move. She suspected that thing would move again any moment now, and she wasn't going to be caught off-guard.

"Audrey," Victoria said softly from beside her.

Audrey started and fell on her ass, eyes wide with nerves as she stared at her friend. Victoria watched her with concern on her face, but thankfully said nothing further.

Faced with four powerful foes, the golem had focused on Audrey. Even though the rest had tried to kill it, its only intent had been to kill *her*.

"Any injuries?" Fyrn asked, eyes on Audrey.

She shook her head. "I'm fine."

Fyrn nodded, apparently not bothered by the golem's appearance, and continued down the now-cleared tunnel as though nothing had happened. Audrey pushed herself to her feet, dusting off her pants as she muttered absently to herself.

"Damn wizards."

CHAPTER ELEVEN

I n the royal master suite, nestled in the centermost
tower of the Fairhaven castle, Luak set his feet on a
grand dining table. The collection of rooms and hallways
the king had occupied alone comprised over ten thousand
square feet and included a waterfall, sauna, a master
kitchen, and several bedrooms—all of which now belonged
to Luak. The suite had been his for several weeks, and even
though he wasn't officially king, he liked the way a royal
could live.

He drank from a goblet carved from the same crystals
used to make denni, which hummed with power every
time his lips touched its rim. It only gave him the smallest
boost, but the sips added up quickly. He all but gloated
with joy and pride, sitting above the peasants as he reveled
in riches and excess.

It was good to be the king.

Someone knocked on his door and interrupted his jubi-
lation, the fist heavy and hard against the wood.

Cautious in these times of changing power, Luak slunk

silently to the door and peered through a strategically hidden gap in the stone to the side of the door. He himself had gotten the king to open the magically sealed door on the pretense of a group of soldiers delivering a message, and had dragged him out. The soldiers were all loyal to Luak, of course, and the message had been that the king would be escorted to the dungeons.

Luak wouldn't fall for the same trick that had ended the previous reign.

Instead of a small army to whisk him away, he saw one of his higher-ranking mercenaries. The Light Elf had his hands on his knees as he gasped for air, but this was a seasoned warrior who wouldn't be fazed by a trip up the stairs. He had apparently run all this way. Whatever this was about, it was urgent.

Luak opened the door without a word, sword drawn to reinforce the image of an imposing king. These mercenaries needed to respect him, always and forever. No signs of weakness, only unbridled power with a penchant for murder instead of mercy.

They would only respect what they feared, which was just the way he liked it.

"Lord Luak, the Rhazdon host has left the city."

Luak nearly backhanded the man for letting her out of the city, but waited long enough to get more information first. "How did she escape? Why wasn't she stopped?"

"I was patrolling the south tunnels with another soldier, sir, since you requested we split our numbers to cover more ground. When I saw them, I sent my patrol partner to tell you while I trailed them to find out where they were going. I found his remains on the way back. Apparently there's another snarx in the tunnels, sir. It got him before he could get to you."

As expected, the mercenary didn't show a shred of emotion at losing a comrade. These elves and ogres were interchangeable, and barely knew each other. They were loyal only to whoever paid them, and they had few, if any, friends.

It was yet another reason Luak enjoyed commanding a mercenary army—they were easy to replace.

Soon he would enlist the citizens of Fairhaven into his army, but that would have to wait until he had more deep-rooted power in the city. When they had no means to defend themselves, he would draft them to fight and die for him whether they wanted to or not.

"Where did she go?" Luak finally asked.

"I was able to listen in on snippets of their conversation, but Fyrn Folly and Diesel Armstrong are powerful. I didn't dare take them on myself."

Ah, so that was where Diesel had gone. Disappointing, since Luak had wanted to see if Diesel would join him. The young wizard was powerful and, according to rumors, easily swayed by women. Apparently those rumors were true. Now, the boy would have to die for supporting Victoria instead of Luak.

"I only heard they were going to Sedona," the mercenary continued.

As much as he hated to admit it, a pang of fear tore through Luak's chest. *Those fools.* They would get Victoria killed in the network of tunnels beneath Montezuma's Well, and Luak would lose his Rhazdon Artifact to the labyrinth. Only a desperate idiot would travel to the remnants of Lochrose.

He paced the expensive suite, hand in his hair as he debated his options. Perhaps it was his fault they had left. He had been too obvious in overthrowing the king, too blatant in the way he had kidnapped, tortured, and killed the senators and generals who needed to either join him or die. That was the downside of moving his plan forward—the subtle nuance of the original timeline was lost.

Still, he had what he wanted. Well, everything except Victoria Brie and her Rhazdon Artifact.

But there was little he could do. There were things even he dared not disturb.

Luak rubbed his temples, mind racing as he tried to adjust. He couldn't simply forgo the Rhazdon Artifact in Victoria's arm. He needed it desperately. It was vital to securing Fairhaven and destroying what little courage the citizens of this kemana might have left after he officially declared himself king.

When their precious hero was killed in front of them, no one would dare to voice dissent. With her execution, their hope would die.

"Find her," Luak said darkly.

"Sir?"

"Go to Sedona. Find Lochrose. Capture her alive. Drug her, knock her out—I don't care, as long as you drag her back here alive. I will give you and everyone in your party four years' salary if you succeed."

This caught the mercenary's attention and he leaned forward, apparently hanging on Luak's every word.

Luak paced the entry while he gave his orders. "Kill the

rest if you have to, but I'll give you another five thousand denni if you bring the other girl back alive as well. I want to kill them both myself."

"But sir, Lochrose is a myth."

"It's quite real, or I wouldn't order you to go, would I?" Luak's eyes narrowed as he glared at the brazen mercenary. "Take ten of the best soldiers you have and travel undetected to Sedona. I will draft a map. Track the girl. Bring her back, or don't return."

The mercenary's eyes widened, but he saluted and retreated without another word.

Luak could warn them of the traps and creatures in the caves, but they would probably desert him. They didn't need to know what was down there waiting to kill them. He merely needed them to drag Victoria Brie to him, begging for her life.

And after even a few nights in the horrors of the Lochrose ruins, she would break. When she arrived on her knees in front of him, she would be begging for death.

CHAPTER TWELVE

L ochrose went on *forever.*
It was astonishing that the route never seemed to change and the walls were always identical. Even stranger was the complete lack of time or any concept of how far they had traveled. It made Victoria uneasy, but she tried not to let it bother her.

She walked with Fyrn as Styx flitted overhead, wondering how to word what she wanted to say.

"Out with it," her mentor said with an impatient sigh.

She frowned. "This Rhazdon Artifact you want us to find... Do you know who the ghost is? What powers are tied to it? How can I prepare? I feel like I'm walking in blind, and I don't like that one bit."

The old wizard's staff tapped rhythmically with his steps. "I don't know the ghost, no. There's no written record of the soul tied to the Rhazdon Artifact we're looking for, since it's been lost for so long. However, it will give you the strength you need to fully utilize the other one."

She lifted one thin eyebrow and stared him down, silently willing him to say more.

He shook his head. "That's all you need to know."

"Like hell it is. Every Rhazdon Artifact has three powers, and this one will be no different. It will give me physical strength, but what else can it do?"

Fyrn studied her with a harsh gaze, similar to the way her high school teachers had stared her down when she spoke out of turn during class. After a second, though, his expression softened. "You're right. You'll find out after fusing with it anyway. I suppose I was merely trying to protect you from becoming power-hungry like—"

"Like the others," she finished for him.

She was the only known Rhazdon host who didn't kill for sport or power. It befuddled the people around her, and though Fyrn trusted her, it was clear he worried about her.

Hell, Victoria was a little worried about herself.

She had a clear mission, and that drove her forward. Deep down, she suspected the other Rhazdon hosts didn't have her focus or her friends, and that was what made her so successful. Her only goal was to protect Fairhaven. Well, and kill Luak along the way. Most Rhazdon hosts would have tried to usurp the throne by now.

But not her, and Fyrn knew it.

Fyrn studied the ground as if it were interesting, obviously letting his mind wander as he spoke. "What we are looking for is a small bear figurine carved of onyx, unassuming to any who don't know its power. It grants its host incredible will in body, mind, and emotion."

Victoria studied his face a moment, confused. "That cryptic wizard-speak may make sense to you, but to me…"

He huffed. "You will have immense physical strength, almost limitless emotional control, and enhanced intelligence. The world and everything in it will come easily to you."

Ah. Thus his hesitation. "And you're afraid the suddenly super-smart me is going to take over the world?"

"A little," he admitted.

She laughed and waved away the thought. "I'm not going to turn evil, Fyrn. Besides, you'll get a suite in the palace if I do."

"Of course she won't turn evil! It would break my heart, and she wouldn't do that," Diesel called from the back of the group.

Victoria didn't roll her eyes. She laughed instead, surprising herself. Diesel's annoyingness had at some point eroded her stubborn dislike of him. At least now he could entertain her a bit. Maybe the thought of losing him had allowed her to forgive his irritating advances.

A little. Just a little.

She cast a backward glance to find Audrey sulking, shoulders tense as she glared at the glimmering walls they were passing.

Victoria's smile fell. "What's wrong, Audrey?"

Audrey's gaze shifted to Victoria without so much as another motion, the sudden movement not unlike watching a portrait's eyes shift. Victoria nearly jumped in surprise, and Audrey seemed to notice she had done something wrong. "Sorry, V. This place gives me the creeps. And, well, that golem—"

"It's dead and it's not coming back, thanks to you," Fyrn said without looking back.

"That was a compliment, in case you missed it," Victoria said with a chuckle.

"Humph," Fyrn said absently.

Audrey, though, didn't crack even the smallest of smiles. "It was going after me."

"It was willing to kill all of us, if you'll recall." Diesel chuckled.

Audrey shook her head. "It never took its eyes off me, except when Victoria cut its arm off."

"She's right," Fyrn said without pausing in his steady gait.

"What? But why?" Victoria slowed until she was next to Audrey, ready to draw her sword if need be to protect her friend.

"Because I'm Atlantean," Audrey answered.

At this, Fyrn stopped and turned on his heel to study her. "How can you be certain?"

"Well, that's what the ghost in my head is telling me, anyway."

Victoria laughed. She couldn't help it.

Fyrn shushed her with a sharp glare and leaned on his staff. "The spirit tied to your Artifact said this?"

Audrey nodded. "Apparently there were wars between Atlanteans and the wizards. Neither liked each other very much."

"That's news to me," Diesel said, spinning his staff like a baton. It was an absent motion, meant more to keep his hands busy than anything else.

Audrey shrugged. "The Atlanteans disappeared, and the largest wizard settlement was all but wiped out. I guess the hatred died with them."

An idea popped into Victoria's mind. "You don't think—"

"I do," Fyrn interrupted. "Perhaps the traitor was not from within after all."

"My kind destroyed Lochrose?" Audrey asked, almost too softly to hear. She sounded heartbroken, and Victoria set a hand on her back for comfort.

"It's possible," Fyrn admitted. "In which case we are going to have to be very protective of you, Audrey. Any other traps or enchantments that remain may target you specifically for your blood, especially now that you're more attuned to your gifts. Any survivors may hate you instantly. You don't exactly look human anymore, and that tiara is a dead giveaway to your heritage."

"But it's just a silver headband."

"That's Atlantean metalwork, child, with an Atlantean crystal embedded in its tip. If there are wizards and witches here, they will know what it is and what you are."

Audrey nearly gulped. "But they aren't, right? There were no survivors."

"There was also not supposed to be a lingering warning cry on the entrance," Fyrn said solemnly.

"Touché," Audrey admitted softly.

"You should practice shifting into a witch, Audrey. You must be ready. If we encounter survivors, you must pass as one of them."

"But the tiara remains on my head when I shift."

"I believe you can hide even that with practice. I urge you to try as we walk."

Audrey nodded. Victoria studied her as the girl nervously balled her hands into fists. She could read her friend easily—Audrey hated this place. It didn't take a genius to realize Audrey wished with all her heart that she could leave immediately. From her expression, everything in her soul told her to flee as fast as her strong legs could carry her.

But after one look at Victoria, a flicker of under-standing crossed her face. She must have realized this was exactly how Victoria had felt in the bowels of Atlantis.

"The shit we do for our friends," she muttered.

"You have no idea," Victoria said with a laugh. She carried on down the tunnel, and the wizards walked after her.

Not long afterward Audrey's soft footsteps followed, and Diesel dropped to the back of the party so that Audrey would never be in the vulnerable spot at the rear.

After a few moments of walking with Styx buzzing around her head, Victoria picked up the distinct sound of chattering voices. They reminded her of Styx, but were higher in pitch. He squeaked and landed on her head, thumping her scalp to get her attention. His soft wings tickled her scalp.

Around a bend, a recess in the tunnel wall let in a trickle of silver light from somewhere overhead. A thin stream of water bubbled over the rock wall in a small waterfall, pooling by a moss-covered boulder.

On the rock sat a tiny creature that reminded Victoria of a fuzzy pink tennis ball with stubs for legs. As she neared, four little ears popped up from within the fluff, all of them focused on her. Seconds later, two massive eyes opened. The black irises covered half the creature's body and it stared at her as though more intrigued than afraid. It cooed.

"Aw, what a cutie," Victoria said softly.

Styx muttered and tugged on her hair jealously, but she waved him away. He fluttered into the air, pouting.

"Nothing could replace you, Styx," she said with a wink to her little companion.

He smiled, blushing a bit, and reluctantly waved her on as if he wanted her to continue complimenting him.

Instead, Victoria leaned in toward the little fluff ball. It bounced once, gaining new footing on the boulder as its adorably massive eyes stared her down.

"What is this?" Victoria asked Fyrn.

To her surprise, the old wizard shrugged. "I haven't read anything of these creatures."

"What? The mighty Fyrn *doesn't know?*" Victoria had to bite back her shit-eating grin as she teased him.

He grumbled and nodded toward Diesel. "Have you ever heard of these creatures? Should we be concerned?"

Victoria quirked an eyebrow. "Concerned? They're adorable!"

Diesel shook his head. "This thing looks somewhat like a snuffle, but those are supposed to be extinct. No one has any drawings of the creatures, only descriptions. One moment...I simply must document this."

Fyrn groaned in annoyance. "This isn't a school trip. I merely need to know if we should kill it or not."

Diesel pulled out his quill and notebook. "This will take only a moment. I'm quite an accomplished artist."

"Of course you are," Audrey muttered.

Victoria stifled a chuckle and neared the endearing

little creature. It cooed softer the closer she got, and she couldn't help but feel grateful to find something sweet in this supposed cave of horrors.

And then her instincts flared for no logical reason. She took a proactive step back seconds before the creature opened a mouth the size of her fist, gums littered with jagged and broken teeth. It lunged for her.

Diesel yelped. "It's not a snuffle! It's definitely not a snuffle!"

Victoria didn't comment. She ducked out of the way with practiced ease, the little monster missing her by inches. Out of reflex she summoned her sword and skewered the fuzzy bastard.

Her hopes for a bit of beauty and kindness in this cave dashed, she dismissed her sword and grabbed the furry little corpse out of the air as it fell. It squished in her hand, not nearly as soft as she had expected.

With a disgusted grunt she tossed the creature to Diesel, who caught it with a grimace. "Knock yourself out."

"Ew," Diesel said as he held the creature between two fingers.

Victoria fumed. First a golem attacked her best friend, and now an adorable creature tried to rip her throat out. What next, a dragon?

She winced, hoping she hadn't just jinxed herself.

Without another word she stormed down the hall, cursing this damned place all the while.

CHAPTER THIRTEEN

This whole "not knowing how much time had passed" thing was starting to grate on Victoria's nerves as much as Audrey's. Styx fluttered overhead, oblivious to her discomfort. He probably didn't fully understand the lack of time in these caves, and if he did, he obviously didn't care.

Victoria walked in step with Fyrn down the jewel-lined corridor. There hadn't been a single fork in the road, nor had there been another landmark since the not-a-snuffle had attacked her.

For all she knew they could be walking in place, and she absently checked the floor for built-in treadmills.

Nothing. Just endless rock.

"Are we there yet?" she asked, intentionally adding a bored teenager inflection to the question.

"Close," Fyrn said.

"How can you tell? I feel like I'm on a treadmill."

Fyrn chuckled. "I imagine this is torture to you. If you were a witch, you would feel the various side passages and the time we've spent walking. There's a reason Diesel is dragging at the rear."

"He's tired? I thought he was guarding Audrey."

"A bit of both, I suppose. If you'll notice, he hasn't said anything annoying for quite some time."

Huh. Come to think of it, Fyrn was right. Diesel must really have been tired if he wasn't hitting on her. Victoria peered over her shoulder. Diesel was walking with one hand in his pocket, the other leaning a little too heavily on his staff while his eyes scanned the cave around them.

He caught her gaze and shot her a charming wink.

She shook her head, about to turn back around when she noticed a slight shimmer at the edges of Audrey's form. The Atlantean pinched her eyes tightly shut, and the tiara on her head slowly began to fade. It blurred like a desert horizon, almost disappearing completely before it popped back into sharp focus. Audrey let out a breath and nearly threw up. Apparently she had held it a bit too long.

"Keep going, Audrey," Victoria said with a smile. "You've got this."

Shoulders heaving, Audrey nodded wearily. Victoria knew these shifts took a lot of energy, but if anyone could master it, Audrey was the best bet.

CHAPTER FOURTEEN

Though Victoria had no concept of time, she imagined it was ages before they abruptly came to a stop at the opening to a massive cavern. The vast expanse stretched forever, and was filled with various islands of rock.

Victoria inched toward the cavern. A carved walkway led down, but beyond the ten-foot-wide path was a forty-foot drop she didn't want to risk.

"Something is wrong," Fyrn said softly. As he spoke, a light-blue glow radiated from the crystal at the tip of his staff. His eyes scanned the darkness.

Victoria did the same, tensed for battle despite the odd grogginess that seemed to come out of nowhere and slow her down as her foot crossed the threshold. Another charm, no doubt.

She scanned the cavern, its many crags and islands lit by the same glowing jewels and gems as their tunnel. The seemingly endless expanse truly made it seem as though space itself had opened up to greet them with a twinkling rainbow of color and pinpricks of dazzling light.

If Fyrn hadn't been on such high alert, Victoria might have savored the beauty of the scene.

Leaving the tunnel to see more of the cavern, they inched out onto a ledge lit by the stones around them. Victoria was careful to keep away from the edge, lest she plummet into the deep shadows beyond. Audrey grabbed the back of Victoria's shirt as if doing so would root her to stable ground, and even Diesel's hand found its way around her waist, though Victoria doubted his motives were as pure.

"We should head back," Fyrn said softly.

Victoria gestured back the way they had come. "Why? The tunnel ended here and you seemed confident this was the route to take, Fyrn. What's wrong?"

"There shouldn't *be* a cavern, Victoria. This shouldn't exist. Even if every twist we took was imperceptible to non-wizards, we've been taking forks in the road since the beginning. Up until this moment, I instinctively knew exactly where to go. Then out of nowhere the tunnel ended here, but that doesn't make sense. The route to Lochrose is one of tunnels, not caverns. Something is very, very wrong."

"Fine, fine. We'll go." Victoria spun on her heel and nearly ran into a cliff wall. She gasped, confused. A second ago there had been a tunnel, and now the way was blocked with rock. She pressed her hands against it, wondering if it were another illusion like the entrance at Montezuma's Well, but the sharp edges nearly cut open her palm.

Fyrn followed suit, pressing his fingers against the rock. "Fuck."

Victoria's brows shot up. "I've never heard you cuss like that before."

"We've never been in this much trouble before." He spun around, staff at the ready for an attack. The landscape that met their gaze was different yet again. The towers and islands of rock had shifted while their backs were turned, and they now faced an entirely new vista.

"Shit," Diesel muttered.

"It *must* be bad if you two are suddenly sailors," Audrey snapped. She drew her sword and crept to Victoria's side, while Diesel stood at the end of the line so as to sandwich the girls with wizards.

"Four little travelers, lost in the shadows," a woman's voice said. It was ageless and eternal, echoing from the depths of the cavern much like the golem's roar had.

"*Fuck,*" Fyrn said again, his grip tightening on his staff.

Oh, this was *not* good.

Victoria summoned her sword, eyes scanning the darkness for something—*anything at all*—that might reveal what they were up against.

A massive shadow stalked past the jewels deep below, but Victoria couldn't quite tell how big it was. Without a proper frame of reference it could be several stories tall or no larger than a lion, though neither thought was very reassuring.

A draft of air blew past her face, and she had the dizzying sensation of vertigo. They seemed to be up high, and if that was true this creature had to be the size of several eighteen-wheelers stacked on top of each other.

"What the hell was that?" Audrey hissed, voice hushed as her eyes darted along the cavern walls.

Fyrn raised his staff, its tip glowing brilliantly as he prepared to fight. "I'm not sure yet, but I'm fairly certain we don't want to know."

The voice chuckled, the sound echoing several times over. "You're correct, old wizard. You do not want to know me, but you will. One by one, I will savor your hot blood between my teeth."

"That's a little dark," Audrey muttered.

"Who are you to criticize the darkness, Atlantean? I quite enjoy the taste of hypocrites."

With that, the shadow deep in the cavern launched itself. It sailed toward them impossibly fast, and Victoria raised her blade seconds before the beast was upon them.

In the chaos time slowed, but still Victoria could barely react fast enough.

To her left, a blinding bolt of light shot from Fyrn's staff. To her right, a white burst of lightning tore from Audrey's palm. Green energy sparked and fizzled from Diesel's staff not far away.

The sudden burst of light illuminated one of the most horrifying things Victoria had ever seen in her life.

A giant woman snarled at Victoria, her beautiful eyes contorted with hatred. Her towering face was easily three times Victoria's height, and a lion's mane flanked her cheeks and temples like flawless strawberry hair.

The red fur along her neck and paws—*paws?*—shimmered copper in the light, and the brilliant blue feathers of her massive wings matched the azure-blue glow of her eyes. She—although whatever the hell this woman was, she was definitely not human—bared her teeth. They were sharp as daggers and she attacked, inches from skewering all four of them with a single bite.

Victoria struck first.

She drove her sharpened blade into the creature's mouth, drawing a rush of blood that spilled like a waterfall onto the ledge where the four stood. It coated Victoria's hands and arms, but she gritted her teeth and drove her blade in farther.

The monster shrieked and batted its wings, pulling itself away from Victoria's blade and fading into the darkness as a barely-visible wraith overhead.

"Hold onto each other!" Fyrn shouted. He struck his staff against the ground as Diesel grabbed Victoria's waist and tugged her close. Before she could push him off, light splintered from beneath the elder wizard's staff and the ground beneath them rumbled as though he had started an earthquake.

The ground gave under them, and they fell.

She and Diesel plummeted down the rocky cliff with nothing to catch them as they fell into the darkness.

A second later Audrey screamed, and Victoria had a split second to be grateful her friend hadn't been lost in the chaos. Her moment of gratitude came and went, replaced by panic, and Victoria couldn't help but scream as well. Even Diesel yelled on their way down, but Victoria couldn't hear Fyrn.

She stretched her neck, her panic worsening. *She couldn't hear Fyrn.*

They landed with a thump at the bottom, all of them rolling away from the base as small rocks continued to fall down the cliff. Not missing a beat, Diesel grabbed her and Audrey's hands and bolted, nearly dragging them behind him. Victoria protested, desperate to find her mentor, but Diesel was too strong.

"I don't see Fyrn!" she shouted.

"He's— Victoria, look out!" Diesel grabbed her, swinging her out of the way of a massive boulder seconds before it smashed to the ground.

He pulled her and Audrey into a tunnel lit by the dim glow of more gemstones in the rock. He pressed himself against the wall and set his arm across Victoria's body, pushing her against the rock as well. Since she couldn't wriggle out of his grasp, she pointed into the cavern's darkness. "I'm not leaving Fyrn!"

"You don't have to," the old wizard said as he ambled around the corner into the tunnel. Though he no longer had his pack, he walked with all the calmness of a man who had merely gone on a morning stroll, not someone who had faced a monster before falling down a cliff.

Victoria let out a sigh of relief and slumped against the wall, heart hammering in her chest. She needed a second to calm down, to catch her breath and—

"No!" the monster shrieked, her shrill voice like nails on a chalkboard as it echoed through the endless cavern. "No one escapes me. No one!"

Fyrn pressed himself against the wall as well, eyeing the tunnel's entrance as the massive shadow bolted past. The shrieking continued as the creature shuffled around at the base of the cliff. It sniffed, reminding Victoria of a dog searching for a toy to rip to shreds.

She shuddered.

With a gentle wave of his hand, Fyrn pointed down the tunnel and silently crept away from the giant pot of crazy kicking up dust in the cavern. Victoria nodded and followed, finally letting herself pause to process what she had just seen.

A sphinx. Having pieced together the puzzling array of the monster's features, she knew exactly what it was. Face of a human. Body of a lion. Wings of an eagle.

A sphinx, no question.

Once again the Lochrose tunnels' wards kicked in, and Victoria lost all sense of time. She might have been traveling for days or merely seconds, but when she looked over her shoulder the cavern was long gone. Only the endless tunnels remained.

Fyrn finally paused and sat in a heap on the ground, wiping his weathered face as he leaned against the wall. "Damn it all. I lost my pack when we fell. All the healing tonics and explosives are gone."

"At least you didn't die," Victoria said with relief.

He shrugged as if he almost preferred that option to losing his precious tonics. Victoria rolled her eyes.

Diesel slumped against the wall, and Victoria followed suit. Audrey, however, paced their makeshift camp. "What *was* that thing?"

Fyrn opened his mouth, but Victoria answered first. "A sphinx."

"Yes. Very good!" Fyrn said with a hint of surprise.

"But what's it doing in a wizard ruin?" Audrey demanded.

"And why did it seem to lose us when we entered the tunnels?" Diesel added.

Fyrn stroked his beard. "I'm not entirely certain, but I believe this has something to do with why we lost Lochrose in the first place. The enchantments on that cavern are powerful. Immortal. Immovable. It is the creature's lair. Whatever magic we fell into is part of the sphinx's defenses, and it ensnares victims by changing the tunnel structure. We should never have arrived at that cavern."

"So we might face it again?" Audrey asked, exasperated.

Fyrn nodded. "I'm afraid so. We must be prepared, though even *I'm* not entirely certain how we could possibly defeat such a creature. I've only faced something that powerful a handful of times in my life."

"That's reassuring," Victoria mumbled.

"We need to rest," Diesel said, his familiar smile long gone. His gaze darted round the tunnel as though something might attack them any moment and he shifted, apparently unable to sit still. If the tunnels to Lochrose and the sphinx in its depths had rattled Diesel out of his joking charm, they were truly in deep shit.

"I'm not tired," Audrey countered.

Diesel shook his head. "You *are* tired, Audrey. I guarantee it. We've been traveling at least ten hours straight, and after that excitement we need a moment to breathe. I've read about the wizard enchantments in this city. They were designed to wear you down until you died of exhaustion. You'd amble through the tunnels with no sense that you needed to sleep. Until today, I never thought such spells were possible."

Victoria shot a knowing glance at Fyrn, who nodded almost imperceptibly. Her mentor always seemed to have the upper hand, and it made her feel a bit giddy to know Diesel was unaware of the secret project hiding beneath Fairhaven. Her mentor had trusted her with something not even the second most powerful wizard in Fairhaven knew.

"I'll keep first watch," Diesel said, leaning against the wall as he peered down one end of the tunnel.

Victoria studied him for a moment. She had never seen him truly rattled, not even when they were on their knees before the Atlantean king. It unnerved her to see him serious.

As if he felt her stare, he turned his head and caught her eye. This time he offered the barest of smiles. "It's okay, Victoria. We're safe."

"For now," she added. With that, his smile fell.

Victoria woke to a fizzling silver light inches from her face. She gasped and pushed herself backward, only to hit her head against the hard rock wall. She grimaced, holding the sensitive place at the back of her skull, and tried to get a sense of what was going on.

A blond man scowled at her. He held the piece of wood that had the light coming from the end as though it were a sparkler. He aimed it at her menacingly, and in her sleepy state she nearly laughed at the ridiculousness of a man trying to hurt her with a sparkler.

Only this wasn't a sparkler. It was a wand.

As she fully woke, the realization crashed into her like a wave. This was a wizard, someone she didn't know.

She scanned their makeshift camp and in the dim light

could make out Diesel bound with glowing white rope between four men, all of whom aimed their wands at him and held a bit of the rope to keep him steady. Diesel glared at the man holding Victoria hostage as though he wished he could reach out and rip him to pieces.

Another six men surrounded Fyrn, and her mentor eyed her warily as if waiting to see what she would do. Styx chattered furiously from a metal cage on the ground, banging his tiny fists against the bars. Two more men surrounded Audrey, who seemed to be holding her breath.

Oh, no. If they find out she's Atlantean, they'll—

But they hadn't killed her yet. In fact, as Victoria studied her friend in the dim light, she realized the tiara was missing from her head.

Audrey had shifted, and she was barely hiding the Atlantean Artifact that would mark her as an instant enemy to these wizards.

The only one left was her...a Rhazdon host. Hopefully no one would lift her sleeve.

The wizard barked an order at her in a language she didn't understand. Baffled, she turned to Diesel, but he shrugged.

Great. Even the know-it-all didn't have a clue what was going on.

The strange wizard gestured for her to stand, and she got the gist. She obliged him, calmly surveying the scene as she strategically lifted her hands in front of her. The wizard would think she was surrendering, but she could easily summon her sword and skewer him if need be.

If these men were powerful enough to overtake Fyrn and Diesel without making enough noise to wake her, she might not stand a chance. However, she had the element of surprise on her side. If she could summon her blade fast enough, perhaps—

"Don't," Fyrn said simply.

Victoria stared at him in astonishment. He nodded calmly, as though he weren't being held captive.

Baffled, Victoria lifted her hands in full surrender. The wrist guards on her sleeves were more than enough to keep the cloth covering her Rhazdon Artifact in place.

The wizard shouted something at her and shoved the wand in her face again.

"That's getting old, buddy," she snapped, glaring at the wand he kept waving in front of her nose.

He shouted at her again and began to pat her down while holding that stupid little wand in her face.

She frowned, about ready to draw her sword and slice the damn thing in two. "Talking louder doesn't make me understand what you're saying!"

"Victoria, comply," Fyrn said calmly.

"What? Why?"

"Trust me, Victoria," was all the old wizard said.

And she did. With a sigh she set her hands on her head and walked ahead of the wizard, exposing her back to someone who had just threatened to kill her.

Fyrn had better have a damn good reason for this, or she was going to beat the ever-loving crap out of him.

CHAPTER FIFTEEN

Victoria trudged through the tunnel with her hands on her head, eyes scanning the half-dozen wizards in front of her and wondering where those behind her were.

Fyrn marched ahead with six wands pointed at him, and the wizard who held both his and Diesel's staffs also carried Styx's cage. Diesel and Audrey had been maneuvered to the back, and in the shuffling of so many feet she couldn't tell where they were.

Whoever these men were, they seemed intent on keeping her in the dark as to where her companions were. Any time she turned around to try to check on her friends, the man at her back shouted at her and gestured for her to face forward.

After an abrupt left turn, the timeless sensation of the tunnels lifted like a fog and exhaustion hit Victoria square in the face. She slowed, her eyes drooping with the sudden need to sleep.

Brilliant light blinded her, and she had to blink several

times to rid herself of the imprints on her retinas before her surroundings would come into focus.

Before her was a magnificent paved square covered in elaborate golden stones, and above her an enormous cavern stretched upward for thousands of feet. Massive honey-colored gemstones covered the entire roof of the cavern, casting warm golden light over everything below. The crystals reminded her of Fairhaven, but these were rounded, like domes protruding from the rock. There were thousands, and each gleamed like a tiny sun.

Beneath the amber crystals was a magnificent palace topped with spires and domes like something out of an Arabian fairytale. The castle was painted in reds and yellows, and each of the hundreds of windows was shaped like a massive keyhole.

On either side of the gold-paved road leading to the castle were ornate homes carved from the rock. They gleamed impossibly bright, as though the gray stone were a façade and solid gold lay within every molecule. People stood on the doorsteps and peered from the windows, and they all stared at Victoria.

While the city was beautiful, the hundreds of scowling faces were not.

Everywhere she looked, a witch or wizard stared at her and her companions. It seemed as though every wand in the city had been drawn and aimed at them.

Victoria wanted to crack a joke to alleviate the tension, but she figured it would only make things worse. She kept her mouth shut.

As their captors led them toward the palace, two elaborate doors swung open on a balcony that overlooked the paved square. A regal woman walked out with an elegant red cloak draped over her thin frame. As she lifted a proud chin, the golden chains on her headdress dangling around her beautiful face and high cheekbones.

The woman said something in a cold voice that sent a shiver down Victoria's spine. She wished she could understand what had been said, but it was in a language that seemed to befuddle even Diesel. His mouth parted as though he were trying to place bits of the dialect.

Victoria shot Fyrn an icy glare, but her mentor's gaze remained focused on the regal woman above them as he spoke. "Your Majesty, I—"

She snapped at him in a harsh voice, again in a foreign language.

Crap, this was going to be more difficult than Victoria had initially thought. If they couldn't even communicate, they stood no chance of solving this diplomatically. She prepared to draw her sword again, though now she wished she had done it in the tunnel when the odds of escaping were more in their favor.

The men who had ambushed them kicked Victoria to her knees in front of what could only be Lochrose's queen, and several other wizards did the same to the rest of her group. She narrowed her eyes in challenge to the woman above her, but they were now vastly outnumbered. If Fyrn had simply let her take care of those men in the tunnel…

Damn him.

The queen raised one slender hand and gestured toward Fyrn, who was already kneeling at the end of their line. He grimaced as if the gesture hurt him, and the queen's eyes glowed white.

"Fyrn!" Victoria tensed and prepared to run to him, her instinct to protect her friends overriding her sense of self-preservation.

"Don't," he said through gritted teeth, face contorted in pain.

Victoria nearly ignored him. She wanted to tackle him out of view of this regal woman who had, with barely a moment's hesitation, begun to hurt one of the most important people in her life.

But for his sake, she waited. She leaned forward, ready to sprint the moment he asked for help. She scanned the wizards guarding them, who all watched her warily.

Good. They *should* be afraid of her. If she had to, she would kill them all to keep her friends safe.

Though it felt like an eternity had passed while Victoria waited for Fyrn to ask for help, his expression slowly relaxed. He hunched over, chest heaving as he let out a long, slow sigh of relief.

The regal woman's eyes returned to normal, and she let out a small *hmm*. "English. What an odd tongue."

Victoria snapped her head to the queen, baffled. Only seconds ago the woman had been unable to speak to them.

The woman pointed to Victoria's mentor. "You are Fyrn, disgraced wizard of the Order of the Silver Griffins, but a wizard nonetheless. You are one of us. You will not die here today."

Victoria's mouth dropped open, and she couldn't help herself. "How is it you can speak our language?"

The queen bristled at the interruption, but her eyes scanned the rest of Victoria's party and noted the general confusion. She nodded to Fyrn. "Along with many other details, I extracted the language from his mind. Lochrose is home to the most powerful witches and wizards on Earth, girl. You should not underestimate our ability. Not ever."

Victoria resisted the impulse to shoot a worried look at Audrey. Obviously the queen hadn't extracted *everything*, or there would have been an instant kill order on the Atlantean in their midst.

"Your Majesty—" Fyrn tried to interject.

"Silence." The woman, apparently their queen, turned to Diesel. He knelt beside Fyrn, glaring at the balcony as though he could destroy it even without his staff. For a fleeting second, Victoria wondered if that were possible.

He shot a wary eye toward her just as the queen used her spell on him. He tensed, grimacing as information was unwillingly dragged out of him too.

This woman was stealing information from the heads of the two most powerful people Victoria knew. Worse, though, was the woman's brazen cruelty. She hadn't let them speak for themselves, but had ordered them dragged before her like criminals.

Victoria and Audrey were not wizards. They would not be welcomed, and she didn't want to find out what they would do when they realized what she and Audrey *were*.

Nervous for Audrey's sake, Victoria risked a peek at her oldest friend. Audrey knelt between Victoria and Diesel, next in line for the assault on her mind. If the queen learned what Audrey really was, it would be game over.

The queen smiled approvingly. "Diesel, master wizard of Fairhaven. It is an honor to have you, but you will understand that I won't release you until I've learned who your companions are."

Diesel cleared his throat. "Your Majesty, I—"

"Wait," the woman said simply. She spoke with authority, as though her word and whims were law.

Hell, down here they probably were.

The queen turned her icy gaze on Audrey, and Victoria did the only thing she could think of.

"That's enough!" she shouted, pushing herself to her feet.

Fyrn lowered his head in frustrated defeat, but Victoria didn't care. If the queen found out Audrey was an Atlantean, there would be blood and a frantic frenzy of spells. There would be a battle, one Victoria wasn't sure they would win. They were simply outnumbered.

Victoria wasn't about to leave her friend's life to chance, even if it shifted the entire city's attention to her in a negative way.

If Victoria had to choose between her own life and her friend's, she would always choose Audrey.

One of the wizards behind her grabbed her wrists, and she landed a vicious kick in his stomach. He doubled over and flew backward, hitting the paving and rolling a few feet. Her attention on the queen, Victoria summoned her sword to save the cruel woman from having to fact-check her identity.

Everyone in the city gasped, but seconds later there was only silence. The wizards who had been poised to grab her stepped back in fear as realization set in.

The queen gasped, one slender hand over her lips as she studied the sword. "A Rhazdon host."

Surprisingly, the words came out more amazed than frightened. Her dark eyes narrowed as she studied Victoria. It was the look of an inquisitive and curious mind, as though she could dissect Victoria where she stood.

Victoria didn't want to give her the chance to try.

"We have done nothing to you," she snapped. "We are trying to *help* you, and you have the audacity to not only kidnap us but infiltrate our minds and force us to our knees like criminals? What kind of a pathetic excuse for a ruler are you?"

"Victoria," Fyrn hissed.

"Enough, Fyrn," she snapped. "You might put up with her bullshit, but I won't."

The queen tapped a dainty finger on her chin. "You said you were here to help us. What makes you think we need it?"

Okay, Victoria had to be honest with herself—she was making it up at this point. She had written more than one English essay analyzing some classic book or another, but most of her time in English class was spent writing horse-shit she knew would get her an A.

She could do this. Probably.

After all, she had a few key pieces of evidence on her side to back up her theory that the witches and wizards of Lochrose not only needed help, but needed it *desperately.* Since that was all she had to go on, she would run with it.

"We're here to slay the sphinx that has trapped you underground," Victoria said.

A murmur erupted through the onlookers, and the queen eyed them with annoyance. Good. Apparently Victoria's hunch had been correct—they were indeed trapped here. That monster wasn't their pet, and it had likely munched on more than a few of their own citizens.

The queen lifted one hand, her elegant cloak sliding up her thin arm as she did so. "You are a Rhazdon host. The only person you help is yourself."

Victoria's shoulders drooped a bit, and she stared at Fyrn. "Why is it that everyone believes I'm completely evil? I'm starting to get offended."

Her mentor nodded once toward the queen, and she got his message. *Focus on our main problem.*

Victoria eyed the woman, but her neck was starting to hurt from craning to see the balcony. "We're here to help you. You can accept it, or let us go on our way. I take it we're the first outsiders to enter your home in a long time —maybe ever. Do you really want to kill us?"

"Possibly," the queen said softly.

"I promise you don't." Victoria tightened her grip on the blade, ready to switch to the shield if she needed to protect herself and her friends. This was the moment of truth. Either they were going to be allowed a private audience with this woman, or a volley of spells and attacks would rain on them.

Even though Victoria didn't want to admit it, the ball was fully in the queen's court. With nothing to do but wait, Victoria kept her gaze locked on the regal woman who eyed her disdainfully from the balcony. Whatever happened next depended on the queen's next words.

At an almost imperceptible gesture from the woman, the glowing ropes around Fyrn, and Diesel fell to the ground. Her friends stood warily, the wizards rubbing their wrists as they eyed the monarch on the balcony.

"Join me," the queen said, and disappeared once more

into the palace. Beneath the overhang, a set of hidden double doors swung open.

Apparently still afraid, the wizards who had captured Victoria's group stood back and gestured toward the door, allowing them to enter on their own.

Victoria helped Audrey stand, but the Atlantean looked about ready to keel over from exhaustion. Holding a shift this long must have been excruciating, especially with the fatigue that had set in after leaving the charmed tunnels.

Audrey simply nodded her head in thanks and hobbled through the door, leaning on Diesel as she entered. Free of the threat of immediate death, he shot a grateful smile at Victoria.

She, however, couldn't celebrate yet. They weren't out of trouble until they left this damned city.

Fyrn walked beside Victoria as they entered the massive double doors. "Never undermine me again, Victoria. You could have gotten us killed. You could have—"

"*You* could have told us the plan," she snarled under her breath, finally putting it all together. "You stopped there on purpose in the tunnels, didn't you? You knew they would find us, but you didn't tell me. We could have been prepared. Instead you let us get captured, and you nearly let them know what Audrey is."

Fyrn's face shifted into an expression she had rarely ever seen on him: surprise. She wasn't sure what had brought it on. Perhaps because she was snapping at him and not letting him lead, or perhaps because she had guessed his plan?

"I trust you, Fyrn, but I will beat the shit out of you if

you ever put Audrey's life in danger like that again." With that, Victoria pressed ahead of him.

Fyrn almost couldn't believe what had just happened.

How quickly the student becomes the teacher.

She was right, of course. He could have warned them, but he had wanted to ensure they slept. They wouldn't get to do much of that in the coming days, and they needed their energy. Worrying about an impending ambush would have left them restless and maybe too tense to surrender believably.

He'd had everything under control—at least until the queen had read their minds.

He hadn't been aware such abilities even existed anymore. To not only see it, but to *experience* it was a gift he would treasure forever. These powers the queen possessed were lost arts. He would have to earn the queen's trust and learn her methods, though he had to be honest with himself—Diesel would most likely win that honor.

But what amazed him most was Victoria. Her confidence. Her sacrifice. She would have died in that gilded square to save Audrey. He didn't have a doubt in his mind.

Victoria was a true leader, one most men would follow into battle and off cliffs. She led with compassion, ferocity, and faith in herself.

Perhaps he needed to turn back now and return to Fairhaven. She had mastered her Rhazdon Artifact's darkness, even if she didn't have full control over its power. If she only ever had this one Rhazdon Artifact, he was suddenly convinced that she would never, in all her life, succumb to greed or bloodlust because of the dark magic in her body.

But if he added a second, he very much risked losing the powerful woman she was becoming.

He sighed in defeat, following her and discarding the thought as quickly as it had come. Without the second Rhazdon Artifact, she would die regardless. No, they had a mission, and they would keep to the plan.

To the end, as the girls would say. Despite his weariness, the weathered old wizard smiled.

CHAPTER SIXTEEN

Victoria sat across an elegant table from the queen, with a glimmering golden forcefield between them. Three dozen guards stood around the royal woman, more likely as a show of force than out of concern for her safety, considering the powerful ward that sliced the table in half.

With Styx newly freed from his metal prison and now gorging on the grapes covering her plate, Victoria waited for the queen to speak and used the time to examine their surroundings. The golden forcefield certainly looked imposing, but she wondered what it actually did.

To test it, she tossed one of the grapes on her plate at the forcefield, and it dissolved in a puff of smoke.

Victoria quirked an eyebrow. "Overkill much?"

The queen tilted her head slightly at the phrase as if she wasn't familiar with what it meant, but shrugged. "I do what is necessary to protect my people and myself. Prove me wrong and I will remove it."

Oh, I'm going to prove you wrong. Just wait. Victoria

129

reveled in the thought of making this woman eat her words about Rhazdon hosts being evil.

Well, *Victoria* wasn't evil, at least. Luak was a total *dick*.

"What do you know of the sphinx?" the queen asked, eyes locked on Victoria.

Victoria waited for Fyrn to interject like he always did, but he didn't. He eyed her, apparently waiting for her to answer this one.

"Not much," she admitted. "Just what I know from legends. They're creatures with the face of a human, body of a lion, and wings of a bird. They're vicious and cruel, but you can win against them by answering a riddle."

"Not that we were offered one," Diesel said bitterly. "I'm quite clever and could have answered it easily."

Victoria nudged him in an effort to make him be serious, but he smiled charmingly instead. God, she wished he didn't enjoy messing with her so much.

The queen's eyes widened, and she momentarily dropped her stately decorum. Her shoulders slumped and she leaned forward in her seat with sheer excitement. "You met it?"

Victoria nodded. "It's ugly as sin."

The queen inhaled as though she were a sixteen-year-old who had just gotten the keys to a convertible. "You met it, and you lived? How is this possible? What did it do to you? Did you go into the cavern? If so, how in the heavens did you *escape?*"

Victoria suppressed the smirk pulling at the corners of her mouth. It seemed the queen had more to her personality than cold commands and a regal presence. For the briefest of moments, they had seen the real woman beneath the royal mask.

A few of the soldiers behind her raised their eyebrows, apparently surprised at the outburst. Seeming to sense their confusion, the queen retreated to a proper position in her seat.

It was clear that Victoria had the upper hand. She and her friends had done something amazing in the queen's eyes, and that meant Victoria had bargaining power.

"What's your name?" Victoria asked plainly.

Fyrn nearly spit out the water he was drinking, and Victoria reveled a bit in his discomfort. Her eyes never left the queen's, who smiled mischievously at Victoria's brazen question. "You haven't met many monarchs, have you, child?"

Victoria shook her head. "Just one."

She had wanted to add that he was an asshole and that she hoped this wouldn't be an emerging pattern with the monarchs she met, but she held her tongue. Victoria didn't want to push her luck.

"I am Queen Angelique, but you may call me 'Your Majesty.'"

Ah. Point taken. Victoria nodded, conceding for the moment to keep the conversation amicable. She had no intention of calling her "Your Majesty" long-term.

A nervous prickle raced down Victoria's spine, and she subtly tilted her head until she could find Audrey in her peripheral vision. Audrey remained at the edge of the conversation, quiet and looking a little faint from holding her shift so long. Her face had gone pale, and she leaned slightly to the left.

Victoria willed her friend to hold on a bit longer. She would get all four of them—five including Styx—out of here as fast as possible.

Fyrn set his goblet on the table and leaned toward the queen. "Your Majesty, please tell us how you were trapped here. It will help us in our," he shot an annoyed glare toward Victoria, "quest to help you."

The regal woman sighed wistfully. "I've lived two hundred years, and yet I've never known life outside the city. We are trapped here by that…that *thing*, and I want it dead. If you kill it, you will be rewarded handsomely. You will be heroes to us, treasured champions who will be remembered for all time. You will never want for wealth or status again in your lives."

Victoria tried not to roll her eyes. Thanks to her parents' inheritance she didn't need the money, nor did any of her friends. When she had told the queen they were there to help, she had made a desperate statement to save their hides. Truth be told, she wasn't indebted to these people. They had threatened those she loved most in this world. Invaded their minds and treated them like criminals.

Though Victoria always strove to protect those who needed it and deliver justice where no one else could, she did not like the Queen of Lochrose one bit.

She wasn't proud to admit it, but part of her wanted to lie or do anything else it took to get the hell out of there without lifting a finger to kill the sphinx.

However, a stronger part of her told her she had to do what was right.

Even if Victoria didn't like that they had treated her like

a criminal, she could understand their point of view. These people had been trapped here for centuries, maybe even millennia, with a deadly monster. Of course they were a little hostile.

She sighed, hating her conscience just a bit in that moment. She already had Fairhaven to save and protect. She didn't need another city under her care.

"Every time my people try to leave," the queen said, "the monster chases them down. Our tracking charms show that they always end up in that cursed cavern, and only one has ever come back alive."

"May we speak to this survivor?" Victoria asked, one finger tapping on her temple as her mind raced.

The queen eyed Victoria. "I'm afraid he will be too terrified to speak to a Rhazdon host, even through this ward."

Victoria rolled her eyes.

The queen sighed. "Since the monster took over the Lochrose tunnels, more monsters have crept in. No tunnel is safe. We have lost control of our home and are forced to live here, in the heart of the realm. In her heyday Lochrose was composed of miles and miles of tunnels, and many smaller cities. We were truly a force to be reckoned with. Why, we even had smaller kemanas on the outskirts of the city, with crystals of their own." She gestured upward, no doubt in reference to the magnificent gems embedded in the cavern ceiling far above them.

"But how did this sphinx get in?" Diesel asked.

A sour look passed Queen Angelique's face, and she glared at Victoria. "My ancestors trusted a traitor, a mistake I do not intend to repeat."

Victoria settled into her chair, all but scowling at the queen's unspoken accusation.

Queen Angelique tapped her slender fingers on her chair's armrest. "We were at war with the Atlanteans."

From behind Victoria, Audrey hiccupped. It must have been torture for her to hold the shift this long. Victoria would have to speed this up. To keep from giving her friend away or putting her on the spot, Victoria pretended to ignore the noise and prodded the monarch to continue so they could get this over with. "And?"

"*And*," the queen said with a hint of indignation, "their entire military invaded. We were tricked. They used portals to infiltrate the farthest reaches of the kemana, and they attacked in droves from all directions. Worse, they carried with them dark magic powerful enough to attract a creature like the sphinx from between the worlds, and those petty bastards opened a portal big enough to let it in. They lost hundreds of soldiers to unstable portals, but they didn't care if it meant destroying us."

Victoria lifted one brow in doubt. She didn't like Atlanteans as a whole, but she was familiar enough with their culture to know without a doubt that they honored each other like family unless one betrayed the many. They would never sacrifice themselves or each other over something petty. They had likely believed Lochrose was a threat and that their lives were worth sacrificing for the good of their fellows.

My, my, my, how history spins lies, she thought to herself.

The queen was lost in her story and didn't seem to notice Victoria's hesitation. "They tossed the dark magic into a cavern, which the monster then made its home. It has been warping our wards and spells ever since, trapping us here. None of us can leave so long as that *thing* remains."

"What was the dark magic the Atlanteans brought with them?" Victoria asked.

The queen stiffened. "I hardly think that's relevant."

Oh, but I do. Victoria had a hunch that she knew what it was, and she glanced at Fyrn to confirm. He nodded once into his drink, almost too subtly to notice.

Diesel set his elbows on the table, hands under his chin as he leaned in with curiosity. "Why don't you use portals to leave?

The queen pursed her lips in annoyance. "To protect ourselves from invaders, we crafted powerful charms to protect ourselves from any portals opening in our city. We can't undo those charms unless we perform a certain ritual beneath every crystal dome in the kingdom, and many of those are in the burned and sacked cities the Atlanteans destroyed. In fact, I suspect many of those crystals are broken, leaking our magic and power into the human world above," she added with a disgusted grimace.

Victoria almost smiled. She wondered if the famous vortexes of Sedona, where there was said to be powerful healing energy, were merely the result of the broken crystals of the vast Lochrose cities.

The queen leaned back in her chair, casting an unexpected glance at the floor. "I do so wish I could send teams to repair each of the crystals and retain our power, but alas...we are trapped."

Victoria hesitated, wondering if the queen was playing the damsel in distress to get them to do her dirty work for her.

"You know what the dark magic is," Victoria said bluntly.

Thankfully, Fyrn didn't bother with a spit-take this time. He had likely prepared himself for this question, and it needed to be asked.

The queen glared at her. "Perhaps. Do you?"

Victoria nodded. "It's a Rhazdon Artifact."

"One you are no doubt here to find," the queen snapped.

Victoria hesitated, wondering how she should play this. Finally, she opted for the truth. "Yes, I am. You need to be rid of a monster, and I need the treasure the monster protects. It seems we have a mutually beneficial arrangement."

The queen tilted her chin upward. "A Rhazdon host seeking another Rhazdon Artifact. I was warned about *people* like you. What you crave is endless power, and you will hunt it to the ends of the Earth. It seems I was right about you after all. You're a monster just like the sphinx."

Victoria slammed her fist on the table and stood, knocking over her chair in the process. Both Fyrn and Diesel flinched, but the queen's cold stare never faltered. Victoria did her best to maintain her composure, but she'd had enough. "You have some nerve, woman. You don't know anything about me. You don't know about the murderer trying to take over my home. You don't know about the dozens, maybe hundreds he's killed to take power. You don't know about the mercenaries who are kidnapping and killing people in the streets. You don't know about the fear my fellow citizens live in every *fucking* day while they wait for someone to save them. You don't know how desperately I want to intervene, and yet I can't. I'm not... I'm not..."

Victoria leaned her hands on the table, eyeing the porcelain dinner plates with their golden trim. She fought back a tear and managed to push down the ball in her throat. When she finally did finish her tirade, it was barely a whisper. "I'm not strong enough."

For a moment, Victoria didn't want to lift her head. She didn't want to know what her friends thought of her outburst, much less the queen. But when she forced herself to look at the monarch, the regal woman's expression had softened. She still sat with her ankles crossed and tucked beneath the chair, both arms draped over the armrests like a goddess in a temple. But her shoulders had relaxed, and she watched Victoria with slightly tilted eyebrows, as though she understood the sentiment all too well.

Maybe she did.

"Your payment will be the Rhazdon Artifact," the queen said softly.

Victoria nodded. "It's more than enough."

"And we will help you," the queen added. She snapped her finger at the soldiers surrounding her, though Victoria had almost forgotten they were there, and all three dozen stiffened to attention.

"That's not necessary," Victoria said with the barest glance toward the ever-paling Audrey. "All we need is information."

Diesel watched Victoria warily, as if he didn't quite agree, but he knew he had little choice in the matter.

"Of course," the queen said. She waved her hand at the guards, and they marched in unison out of the throne room. The queen, however, didn't stand, and Victoria had the feeling their conversation wasn't yet done.

"Yes?" Victoria asked when the last guard had left.

The queen took a deep and steadying breath. "Whatever you need, short of people, we will provide. You will not speak to my citizens, only to the soldiers. I do not trust you, Host, but I see that we need each other."

Victoria nodded, assuming that was the end of it, but the regal woman stood. She was taller than Victoria by a few inches, and yet she stared down at her as though she were still on the balcony. "And, human girl, if you betray me once you have the Rhazdon Artifact, I will destroy my city if that's what it takes to end your life."

Victoria quirked one eyebrow, unfazed by the threat. "That's not a very strategic survival method," she said curtly.

With that she marched out of the room and into the street with her friends and the pixie close behind her.

Diesel leaned in, and Victoria tensed for bad news. Maybe the guards had circled back. Maybe this was a trap. Maybe—

"I've fallen in love with you all over again," the obnoxious wizard said in her ear.

She groaned, but couldn't suppress the smile that tugged at her lips. If he could be an idiot again, the danger had truly passed.

Thank-freaking-goodness.

CHAPTER SEVENTEEN

When they reached the tunnels and left the Lochrosian guards at the entrance to the city, Audrey all but collapsed with relief and exhaustion.

To be honest, she hadn't listened to most of what Victoria and the queen had been talking about. The entire time, she had silently begged for it to be over. Holding a shift was hard enough, but to do so under the pressure of death and with no idea for how long... She had nearly passed out. Only her koi had kept her rooted and focused, and it had come at the expense of all other things, like talking, focusing, and sometimes breathing.

"Jesus, monologue much?" she snapped at Victoria once she had her breath back.

Victoria set her hands on her hips as Styx snuggled into her hair. "'Thank you for saving my life, Victoria. You're the greatest, Victoria. You're so pretty and I like your hair, Victoria.'"

"Thank you," Audrey spat impatiently, struggling not to pass out. White and black dots threatened the corners of her vision with every gasping breath. She sucked in air, cleared her head, and calmed her selfish Atlantean blood long enough to say it genuinely. "Really, Victoria. Thank you. They would have killed me."

Victoria nodded once, her expression relaxing. "I would have never have let that happen, Audrey."

"I know." Audrey smiled and relaxed against the wall. She needed to sleep off the fatigue, and even being in the enchanted tunnels didn't assuage her exhaustion. She closed her eyes and let sleep take her.

Victoria watched Audrey as she curled up against the pack the Lochrosians had given her. If she was able to fall asleep that fast, the whole ordeal had been even worse than Victoria had thought. Audrey had to have become incredibly strong, if she had held on for so long.

Styx hummed happily from within Victoria's locks, his hands weaving her hair like the strands of a willow until he had crafted a place to sleep. Too bad, because she needed to sleep too, and he would have to move or be crushed when she laid down.

Diesel set his newly-filled pack on the ground and rummaged through it. Even though he didn't need it, he had refused to let go of his staff after it had finally been returned to him, and it swung about as he sifted through the bag's contents. "They gave us enough food to last a month, and maps of everything they have. Queen Angelique wasn't kidding when she said we would have everything we needed."

"Do they know where the Rhazdon Artifact is?" Victoria asked.

Diesel rummaged through a few of the parchments in the bag. "I think so, my love. At least vaguely."

Victoria shook her head at his pet name. Hopefully she would learn to ignore it in time. He had once said he liked it when she played hard to get, so maybe ignoring him completely would bore him enough to shake off his advances.

Ha, right. When hell freezes over.

It was too much to hope for, but she would try it anyway.

"You did well, Victoria," Fyrn interrupted. The old wizard leaned against his staff, a small smile on his face.

Victoria hesitated, but ultimately smiled back. "Thank you. But please, Fyrn—don't gamble with our lives like that again. I won't trust you any more if you do."

Fyrn nodded. "I apologize. I had my reasons for what I did, but I didn't take into account the queen's power. She is frightening, and yet you faced her as an equal. You should be proud, Victoria."

Her smile widened and she nodded to him once in thanks. They didn't need to say anything more. Besides, Fyrn wasn't the sentimental type. That she had gotten this much from him was truly a gift.

"We should probably begin here," Diesel said, handing Victoria one of the maps and pointing to a small circle in the top right. He leaned in, most likely in an attempt at an intimate gesture, and Victoria did her best to simply disregard it as he continued. "It's the suspected inner lair, the space where the cavern no longer shifts—or at least not as much. It won't change every time we turn our backs like last time."

"Quite the contrary," Victoria said with a yawn. "I think we should start with a nap. Fyrn, you promise to not let us get caught this time?"

The old wizard shook his head, grumbling to himself as whatever tender moment they had shared began to fade. "Lazy woman."

"I heard that," she said, crossing her ankles as she lounged on the floor. It wasn't a featherbed, but after everything they had endured thus far she didn't care.

Audrey was starting to get used to the absence of time within the tunnels. It gave her a sense of harmony and immediacy, a feeling that nothing existed outside of the *now*. She smiled more, despite the oppressive darkness, and found a startling new sensation in her chest. Peace.

It was weird as hell.

She was the feisty one. The jackass. Peace wasn't exactly her thing, but she went with it.

The tunnels mostly wove on and on in an endless gem-lit stretch, but they were treated every now and then to an alcove or even a small meadow illuminated with other-worldly light. Audrey suspected it was merely a leak from above, but with all the darkness it looked like a slice of heaven was shining through.

She shook her head at the thought. *What's with all this flowery shit?*

In her mind, the koi chuckled. *I suppose inner peace isn't for everyone.*

Audrey laughed. Nope, definitely not. She couldn't wait until she had her gym and her sense of time back again.

Victoria, now at the head of the group, lifted her hand to warn them they should be silent. She hid behind a boulder and peered around a bend, and Audrey followed suit. She peered over her friend's shoulder to find another small meadow illuminated by a few thin rays of golden light that filtered through from overhead. This time the clearing was filled with knee-high deer that had two tube-like ears and a long snout. Their tiny tails flailed back and forth, and they chittered to each other as they maneuvered over the mossy floor and nibbled on it as though it were grass.

"Maybe we should shoot one," Diesel said.

"We have more than enough food," Victoria said with a shake of her head.

"Perhaps we do for now, but we could easily be down here for weeks, if not months. We should conserve the rations."

Victoria shrugged. "Fair point, but with what we've seen so far, that could be a special breed of deer whose sole purpose is to poison wizards."

"Or Atlanteans," Audrey added, considering her luck thus far with the wizards of Lochrose.

"Right, exactly," Victoria said with a chuckle. "So you can go ahead and cook it for me if you're feeling generous."

"Of course, my love," Diesel said with a wink. He stood, and she smacked his side until he knelt again.

"I was kidding, obviously," she snapped.

Audrey chuckled.

When the two wizards stood and continued down the tunnel, Audrey tugged on Victoria's sleeve. Her friend spun on her heel, concern on her face, but this wasn't anything serious. Audrey had merely been processing something since their time in Lochrose, and she had to speak her peace. "When we were returning home after escaping Atlantis and General Cato, you told me being a host wasn't all that great. I didn't believe you."

Victoria laughed. "I believe you said hosts were all adored, actually."

Audrey sighed at the stupid comment. "I did, and I'm sorry. I know I wasn't on my game back there, but now I realize the danger you were in, too. If I had known what it was like to be you, what it was *really* like, I never would have asked for this. Truly."

Victoria pulled Audrey into a tight hug. "We have each other, Audrey, and I'm going to need you once I have multiple Rhazdon Artifacts. We know nothing about the ghost tied to this next one, nor do we fully understand its power. Promise me you'll always be there to help me, even if it's to slap some sense into me?"

Audrey laughed. "I will most definitely be there for you if slapping is involved."

Victoria chuckled but continued after the wizards, who had paused to wait for them and watch the deer. The deer, to their credit, didn't seem to care about the strangers' presence.

Audrey, meanwhile, hung back and watched her friends pool by the creatures. Diesel tried to put his arm on Victoria's shoulder, but she smacked it away. He chuckled.

Why do people hate Victoria so much? Audrey wondered. Very few people had bothered to learn who she was or even ask basic questions to understand her motives. Audrey had seen it for herself in Lochrose, and that kind of blatant hatred was scary.

Fear twists even intelligent minds, the koi's soft voice interrupted her thoughts.

"I suppose so," Audrey said softly as she joined her friends.

CHAPTER EIGHTEEN

Victoria was about fed up with this "not knowing what time it is" bullshit. She wanted out of these caves, and fast.

Too bad it hadn't worked that way. She tried to ignore her growing impatience and just let things happen. They would get there when they got there, regardless of how anxious she was to kill this sphinx.

"We're at the inner cavern," Fyrn said softly as he lifted one hand in a gesture for them to slow down.

"Finally." She paused as the tunnel ended in a steep drop. They waited at the entrance, and she peeked around the edge without sticking her head over the threshold. The gentle slope of the wide trail cut into the cliff face to her left and led down into the abyss.

After the disaster last time, they needed a game plan before they charged in with all guns blazing.

The gentle hum of Styx's wings buzzed in the tunnel as he did laps overhead out of boredom. She debated telling him to stop, but it kept him out of harm's way.

Victoria peeked over her shoulder at Audrey. "Do you have your mojo back?"

Audrey nodded and gave a mock salute. "Ready to shoot laser beams, ma'am."

Victoria chuckled. "Laser beams, huh?"

"You're just jealous."

Fyrn stroked his beard as he surveyed the cavern. "Audrey won't be able to use her Atlantean magic while she's shifted into a witch, so we should only have her shift if absolutely necessary."

"Noted," Audrey said. "Only shift upon threat of immediate death by the wizard army."

"Pretty much," Fyrn said with a grumble.

"We need to find the Rhazdon Artifact." Victoria scanned the darkness, hoping something would give it away. A glint of light among the shadows, maybe or—

"There," Diesel said, his hand on Victoria's shoulder as he pointed off to the side. He didn't remove it after he spoke, and she shook her head in annoyance. She needed him to focus.

Staring down his finger, she noticed a few amber rays of light streaming over an apparently empty pedestal. Her heart skipped a beat in panic. "Someone already took it."

Fyrn shook his head. "It's small, Victoria. Barely the size of a ping pong ball. I assure you the Rhazdon Artifact is still here, because the creature is still alive."

Victoria breathed a sigh of relief. "We need a plan to get to it undetected. That thing will likely know we're here the moment we step into the cavern."

"We could set up a diversion somewhere else," Diesel suggested.

Victoria thought it over. "That's not a bad idea."

"It's a risky one," Fyrn interjected.

"How so? A diversion would keep its attention away from whoever steals the Rhazdon Artifact."

"Yes, but at the expense of lives. Once you enter the outer lair, there's a risk of never returning. The fact that we got out at all is luck."

"And my quick wit," Diesel said with a grin.

Fyrn stared at Diesel, head shaking with annoyance, but he continued as if the younger wizard hadn't spoken. "Whoever acts as our diversion will likely die. With the creature on their tail and an ever-shifting cavern confusing them, they could be lost forever in its depths or just flat-out killed. Even if they live and we somehow kill the beast, we might never find them."

"Oh," Victoria and Diesel said in unison.

"Whatever we do, we have to do it in here," Fyrn said with a gesture toward the inner lair.

Victoria tapped her finger on the nearest boulder as she tried to think up a plan. "That's tricky. This area is much smaller, and the monster is massive."

"This inner cavern is larger than it looks," Fyrn said with a gesture toward the map in her hand. "There are corridors and hidden chambers within the lair where our volunteer distracters could lead the sphinx."

"Why doesn't this sphinx tell riddles? In the lore, they have to let you by if you solve their riddle." Victoria chewed her lip in anticipation, a plan starting to form.

Fyrn shook his head. "That's human lore. Fiction. The reality of it is, these are brutes who want nothing more than supper. They have no laws or moral code, much less a desire to play word games with their food."

Damn. There goes my plan.

"Why haven't we seen it yet?" Audrey asked. Her jaw tensed, and her hand inched toward the sword at her belt.

Victoria nodded, equally concerned. She didn't like the quiet, not when that creature was out there somewhere in the shadows.

"It may be patrolling its outer lair," Fyrn said with a shrug.

"What if we go for it?" Audrey asked with a nod toward the pedestal.

Fyrn stroked his beard. "I doubt it will be that easy. We will have to move exceptionally fast and keep to the path on this map. If we deviate even a little, the illusions and shifting floors of the inner lair could make it impossible to leave."

"No pressure," Audrey added sarcastically.

Victoria sat up straighter. "Can you summon the Rhazdon Artifact magically? Make it float up here?"

"I'd have to be closer," Fyrn said, shaking his head.

Diesel grinned. "I know it seems as though we can do anything, my darling, but even great wizards like me have limits."

Victoria shut her eyes in irritation, trying to clear her head and focus even if Diesel wouldn't.

"How close do we need to get?" she asked.

"Twenty feet, give or take," Fyrn answered.

She nodded, a new plan forming. "Audrey and I will be the distractions. You two need to get as close to it as you can, swipe it, and run back. When we see you retreat, we will too. Once the Rhazdon Artifact is secured, we all need to attack the creature with whatever we have to make sure it's kept at bay until—"

She stopped talking mid-sentence and sighed, already disgusted with herself. She was going to say, "until we escape," but that would mean going back on her promise to Queen Angelique. She might not have admired the woman, but she refused to lie.

Diesel seemed to read her mind. "We can steal the Rhazdon Artifact, train you on how to use it, and then go back for the sphinx once you have more power."

Victoria shook her head. "Someone has to die to allow me to fuse with the Rhazdon Artifact, remember?"

Diesel's smile faded, and his gaze flickered to the arm where her dagger was embedded. "I sometimes forget that detail, at least with you."

Victoria didn't appreciate his advances, but he was still her friend—and she didn't like the haunted expression on his face at the thought of someone dying for her to have this power. "Diesel, it's not like that—"

"She didn't kill for that Rhazdon Artifact, Diesel," Fyrn interrupted. "Not that it's your business."

Diesel cleared his throat and plastered on another charming smile, and Victoria was surprised she could tell it was fake. She had been spending too much time around him, and it bothered her how much she hated to think he thought less of her.

"Victoria," Fyrn said sharply.

She tilted her head toward him, fists clenched with the desire to fix whatever she had done to upset Diesel. "What?"

"We will find someone who deserves to die. A criminal. A murderer. Then we will return, and you will keep your promise to Lochrose. Does that suit you?"

She nodded.

"Good. Ready?" Fyrn asked, standing.

"Ready," Audrey said, an Atlantean crystal in one fist.

"As am I," Diesel said, spinning his black wizard's staff.

Victoria stood as well. "Let's do this, then. Styx, are you joining us?"

The little pixie hovered in front of her face and saluted, his tiny features scrunched and exaggeratedly serious. She chuckled despite the dark mood. "Make sure Fyrn and Diesel get the Rhazdon Artifact. If they drop it, you grab it and come back here."

He squeaked in affirmation, apparently ready to perform his duties.

Victoria stretched her arms a bit, readying for the onslaught. "We do this together. One. Two."

"Three," a haunting voice said.

Before they could move an inch, an eye as tall as the cave exit appeared, blocking their way into the inner lair.

Victoria swallowed a scream, and everyone jumped backward.

"Hello, little dinners," the echoing female voice said.

"Retreat!" Victoria shouted.

Audrey shot a brilliant blast of light that caught the monster in the eye. It shrieked in pain, and the wizards covered their retreat with a few well-placed spells aimed at the sphinx's face.

To her astonishment, the sphinx didn't shield its face as the attack ravaged its head. Instead, it reached for its neck.

Its neck must be vulnerable! Her heart leapt with joy at the thought, and she skidded to a stop. She scanned its neck, about to strike when the creature shook off the pain and glared at her.

Apparently her revelation would have to serve her in a future battle. Right now the sphinx had the upper hand, and Victoria had to get her group the hell out of reach.

Breath caught in her throat and thighs aching from stress and a lack of sleep, Victoria led their small band back down the corridor. Seconds later, a long paw topped with razor-sharp claws swiped into the tunnel. The claws dug up rock, gouging the entrance like a knife through butter.

Foiled, the creature put its mouth at the entrance and roared. In the tiny space, the overpowering sound knocked them off their feet.

"This way!" Fyrn charged toward solid rock, and for a moment Victoria thought he had lost his mind. But he disappeared through the wall and out of sight, and Victoria realized this was another illusion. She charged after him, with Diesel, Audrey, and Styx hot on her heels.

The side tunnel looked identical to all the others, and Fyrn led them quite a ways down it before he paused, shoulders heaving, to catch his breath.

Apparently out of harm's way, Victoria slumped against the wall in defeat. She wanted to pull out her hair and hit her head against something. This creature seemed to know everything. Every breath. Every move. It owned these caverns, and it knew all that happened within them.

"I will have you first, Atlantean!" the monster screamed, its voice muted through the rock.

"Aw, I feel special," Audrey said with a forced laugh.

Victoria tensed, ready to run again, but Fyrn shook his head. "We can stay here. If it knew where we were, it would have attacked already."

"Oh, good. I feel safe now." Victoria rolled her eyes. She groaned and slumped on the ground, thoroughly frustrated. "Okay, guys. What's Plan C?"

CHAPTER NINETEEN

The mercenary knelt at the entrance to Lochrose, a vague sense of unease settling deep in his gut as he studied the rocky floor of the gem-filled corridor. There were dark creatures in these tunnels. He knew that much, and he did not want to meet them.

He also wouldn't survive disappointing Luak, thus his dilemma. Option A led to certain death, while Option B led to danger and possible reward.

Option B it is.

"Move," he said, shoving their kidnapped wizard forward.

The barefoot man stumbled, his hands bound in front of him as he led them through the tunnels. "O-of course."

The mercenary gestured to the myriad hired orcs and elves behind him, and they followed his silent command. *He* had surprise and a small army. The Rhazdon host he hunted had nothing more than two wizards who were out of their league.

He would win.

Only a wizard could navigate these paths, and the mercenary didn't like the fact that he had to rely on a prisoner's word. However, he didn't need to threaten their captive anymore. They had shattered his will to fight, and he was now obedient. The broken wizard knew the price of not doing as he was told.

Pain. Lots and lots of pain.

The mercenary had a single mission: find these girls Luak wanted and drag them back to Fairhaven. That Rhazdon host had dark magic in her blood and a shiny little sword, but she now had far more to fear than some monsters in a cave.

CHAPTER TWENTY

Victoria wanted to join in the discussion of what to do next, but she mostly just stewed in her own anger. Styx petted her hair and cooed softly, but the tiny strokes did nothing to stem her fury.

It was bubbling over. Her frustration at being stuck with the Rhazdon Artifact in the first place, her inability to wield the power her father had given her, and the way Luak continuously chipped away at her city despite all her efforts. And no matter what she did to prove otherwise, almost everyone she met in the magical world assumed the worst of her.

Every. Fucking. Time.

Rhazdon hosts are evil. That was the universal rule.

Ha. As if it were that simple.

"Victoria?" Fyrn asked, as though he were waiting for her input on a question.

"Maybe this is all a mistake," she said softly, with no idea what he had asked.

"What?" Diesel sat upright. Audrey leaned forward, apparently as dumbfounded as he was.

Victoria stood and paced in circles around the group's makeshift camp. "Maybe getting a second Rhazdon Artifact really *is* a mistake. Maybe it will make me evil. Maybe coming here and promising the impossible to some asshole queen was the worst thing I could have done. Maybe—"

"Maybe you're afraid she's right," Fyrn interrupted.

Victoria stopped dead in her tracks and stared at her mentor. For a moment she couldn't speak, but the anger bubbled once more to the surface. She had to swallow hard to stem the tears. "Why the hell does everyone I meet think I'm a monster? She didn't even ask why we were here, Fyrn. She didn't care. No one cares!"

"They don't understand."

"Are you sure, Fyrn? I mean, why am I *not* evil? By all accounts I should be. All the rest are, right? Rhazdon. Luak. I'm sure there are loads more. Am I going to slip into madness or something? Should I buy a hut in the woods so I don't rampage? What makes me different? Who am I to think…" she trailed off, tears springing to her eyes as she fought to finish that statement.

"I don't know how, but you're not evil. Not even a little," Fyrn answered.

"Not yet."

His jaw tensed, but he nodded. "Not yet. Maybe not ever. We don't know."

"You don't *know*." She echoed his words, her voice so soft she almost couldn't hear herself. His confession broke her heart. She rubbed her eyes to stem the frustrated tears as she reevaluated her entire life's purpose.

"Maybe it's in your blood," Fyrn said. "Or maybe it's the way you got the Rhazdon Artifact—through a sacrifice to save your life, rather than greed on your part. Some scholars debate that the ghosts tied to the Rhazdon Artifacts can impact the host's experience in more profound ways than we understand, but I doubt that in your case. Shiloh is rather useless."

"I heard that," Shiloh said from somewhere in the shadows.

Victoria waved him away. "You wouldn't be useless if you were more helpful and appeared with at least *some* regularity."

"Humph," the ghost said quietly.

With a sigh, Victoria plopped onto the nearest boulder, shoulders drooping. "Maybe I just haven't been a host long enough for the darkness to take hold."

Audrey stood. "Victoria, you said I could slap you around if I needed to, and I'm about to if it means I can knock some sense into your brain."

Victoria frowned and sat up, confused. "Audrey, this is serious. This might be out of our control."

Audrey leaned toward Victoria's face until Victoria had no choice but to look her friend in the eye. "You are a fighter, and you will not go down quietly."

"I—"

"*Are you evil?* Jesus. No! You're not! You saved a city from a snarx. You saved me from Atlantis. At every turn, you are kind and protective. If you're evil, that's the kind of evil I want in my life. If that's evil, evil is the *shit* and I love it."

Victoria sat a little straighter, debating the words, and

let them sink in. A slow smile spread across her face, and she wiped away a final tear. "Thank you. And you did it without any slapping at all."

"Oh, I wouldn't say that." Audrey smacked Victoria on the cheek hard enough to sting.

"Ow! What the hell!"

"That's for doubting yourself. Don't do it again." Audrey nodded, apparently satisfied with herself.

Victoria rubbed the welt, but she accepted it all the same. "Fine. *Ass*."

"You're welcome." Audrey returned to her seat. "So, we have a second Rhazdon Artifact to steal and a sphinx to kill."

Victoria laughed. "Damn right we do."

"What's the plan?"

Victoria leaned back against the cave wall, her hope renewed. "Let's figure something out. I think its neck is vulnerable, so we'll start there. Any ideas?"

Diesel raised his eyebrows suggestively. "I have loads of ideas when it comes to the neck. Shall we try a few?"

Victoria rolled her eyes, but she couldn't suppress her smile. "You're an idiot."

While the other three laughed, Fyrn leaned against the wall in contemplation. In truth, Victoria had voiced his darkest fear.

In his core, Fyrn nursed a lingering thought that would not leave him however hard he tried. He hoped she would never lose herself to newly acquired power. All the rest had. Why not her?

She was kind and compassionate. If he left things as they were, she would stay that way.

He watched the young woman he had taken on as a student and, if he were honest, a daughter. She laughed in the low gemstone light of the tunnel, and he answered his own question.

Why *not* her? Because she was Victoria Brie, and not even the darkness would win against her.

He smiled, truly happy for the first time in decades. When did he become such a sentimental old fool?

CHAPTER TWENTY-ONE

Victoria woke with a start, sitting upright as she struggled to catch her breath.

Across from her, Diesel sat still as a stone. It must have been his turn to keep watch. He studied her as though she had startled him, and perhaps she had.

Panic flooded her body as though someone were attacking her, but she still lay on the floor of the cave in a bedroll from the pack Queen Angelique had given her. Audrey and Fyrn were in their bedrolls on either side of her. Diesel's bedroll was still tucked in his bag, waiting for his turn to sleep.

Despite the stillness, something was terribly wrong. Victoria just didn't know what it was.

She stood, her body flooding with adrenaline she didn't understand. It was as though something were crouching in the shadows just out of reach. The sensation reminded her of the times she wove through the tunnels on her way to their safe house in Fairhaven, something hot on her heels the whole way.

But this was worse.

Far worse.

"Get up," she hissed to Audrey and Fyrn. The two stirred, but neither opened their eyes.

"Victoria, what—" Diesel said.

"I don't know, but we need to go. Now."

"Where?"

"Anywhere but here."

"But—"

"Hello, little dinners," a familiar echoing voice said from the darkness.

"It seems the creature found you," Shiloh said. The ghost was suddenly beside her.

Already jumpy from nerves, she spun on her heel to face him with a bite of sarcasm in her voice. "That was *almost* helpful. Thank you."

He offered a lazy bow and disappeared.

The creature roared, and the shrill scrape of claws against the rock wall screamed through the tunnel. Pebbles tumbled from overhead, and Victoria nudged Audrey one more time as the heavy sleeper finally woke. She hopped out of the bedroll and tucked it under her arm, barely bothering to fold it as she grabbed her bag.

"We have to go!" Victoria shouted. They raced through the tunnel, and the grate of claws on rock followed them.

"I thought it couldn't sense us in the tunnels!" Audrey shouted as they ran.

"These are *my* tunnels," the eerie voice answered. "It merely takes time to find my food in here."

"Great," Victoria said with an eyeroll.

A rock fell from overhead, and Victoria pulled Diesel

out of the way at the last second. He shot her a flirtatious wink as they bolted past the boulder, and she supposed that would have to suffice as her thanks for saving his life.

Around a bend, a gaping hole in the tunnel exposed them to the inner lair beyond. It was as though a hole to space itself had opened before them, and a thought occurred to Victoria—this thing had been hunting them. As soon as it had broken open the tunnel wall, it had shattered the Lochrosian enchantment on the tunnel and destroyed the magic that had hidden them.

Shit.

Teeth appeared in the opening, the lips stretched wide as the disgusting thing grinned in victory. It roared from barely thirty feet away, and the force of the sound knocked Victoria backward.

Off-balance, Victoria dropped everything. This thing would eat them. It would rip them apart and kill the people she loved most.

Like *hell.*

She had only her empty hands and her instinct, so Victoria acted on impulse. Using her training as fuel, she jumped toward the sphinx and summoned her sharpest sword, digging it into the beast's open mouth as it ferociously clawed at the opening.

The moment her blade sliced open its tongue and gums, the sphinx screamed the loudest it had so far. Victoria's ears rang. It thrashed like a snake, desperate to get away, and Victoria fell. She hit the floor hard and rolled, sliding the last few feet out of reach.

The massive head snaked backward until its icy eyes

zeroed in on her. Its copper mane flailed like Medusa's hair, wild and untamed.

"You are *food*," it growled.

"No, I'm *pissed*," Victoria corrected.

On a whim and, with full trust in her Rhazdon Artifact, she summoned a throwing knife. She tossed the blade at the beast's nearest eye, and it struck. The sphinx clawed at the wound and slid out of sight.

Victoria raced to the edge, ready to strike another blow. As she neared, a blast of air hit her in the face. Her hair danced around her head as she stared down an impossibly steep cliff face. Gouges in the rock betrayed where the sphinx had tried to regain its footing as it fell into the darkness.

Victoria closed her eyes for the briefest of seconds and called her weapon back to her, and a weight settled into her hand. Sure enough, the throwing dagger had appeared on command.

She smirked at the beast lost somewhere in the shadows of the cavern floor. In the darkness, one glowing eye seethed up at her, the other one probably sealed shut from the wound.

In a flash, it disappeared. She scanned the valley below, desperate to track it.

There.

A massive shadow tore past the islands of rock in the inner cavern, occasionally blocking out glowing gemstones in the wall. It seemed to be heading toward the glimmers of golden light in the far corner.

Its loot.

"Victoria, that was amazing!" Audrey patted Victoria on the back.

Victoria offered a small smile in thanks, but her mind was elsewhere. Bit by bit, she pieced together the information she had picked up thus far and began to make educated guesses about the rest.

"See, I was helpful," Shiloh said from behind them.

Victoria raised one eyebrow in challenge. "Warning me that the sphinx had found me *after* it made itself known wasn't helpful."

"I woke you up," he said simply.

This caught Victoria's full attention. "That panic feeling was you? Why didn't you just talk to me?"

"You yell at me every time I do that."

She crossed her arms, waiting for a better answer.

He shrugged. "In your dream state, you can't converse. I had to speak with emotion."

"You can feel emotion?" Audrey asked.

Victoria elbowed her friend in the ribs.

The ghost elf studied his fingernails. "Anyway, you're not dead. Good job, I guess."

"Shiloh?" Victoria asked.

He paused and looked up at her, obviously waiting for her to yell at him again.

"I like it when you're helpful. Thank you," she said instead.

He nodded, apparently bored with the whole conversation, and disappeared into thin air.

Darn. She had hoped for a smile or something. Oh, well. Diesel and Fyrn leaned against the cave wall, conversing in hushed voices while Audrey stretched and smiled as though they had won some great battle.

They hadn't won anything. The creature would be back.

Victoria's thoughts raced as she tried to put together the final piece of the puzzle: why the sphinx cared about dark magic at all. Perhaps the monster gained power from the Rhazdon Artifact in some other way than a host would. Perhaps the magic could heal it or make it stronger, and thus the sphinx coveted the item and had raced to it when injured.

Regardless, Victoria now had a far better idea how to defeat this creature once and for all. But to do it she would need a little help, and Audrey wasn't going to like this one bit.

CHAPTER TWENTY-TWO

"This is an absolutely terrible idea," Audrey seethed, her voice a whisper as they snuck through the palace halls.

Victoria shushed her. It was too late to argue.

The four of them moved through the darkened hallways, Fyrn and Diesel using every sneak and glamour spell they had ever learned to mask their steady approach to the queen's chambers.

Similar to Fairhaven's green crystals, the amber-colored stones powering Lochrose dimmed to simulate night. Victoria had waited until the darkness gave them shadows to run through, offering them a better chance to infiltrate the castle.

Right on time Styx flitted from around the corner, gesturing wildly to the left. Apparently he had found the room they were looking for.

Victoria almost released a sigh of relief when the glimmer of glowing wand tips appeared at the far end of the hall. Without a word, Fyrn cloaked them in a shimmering mist. Victoria held her breath, and Audrey gripped Victoria's shirt as though it were a substitute for throttling her.

The pair of guards walked by, muttering in the language she didn't understand, and turned down the hall to the right. Above them, Styx hung onto a chandelier to keep anyone from hearing the buzz of his wings, just as Victoria had asked.

She gestured to her companions, and the march resumed. They didn't have long.

The more Victoria had thought about it, the more it had seemed like the queen was hiding something from her—something very important. Something without which Victoria couldn't kill the sphinx that had trapped the people of Lochrose in their homes.

But it didn't make sense. They had an agreement, and the queen had promised to give Victoria anything she or her small group needed.

Well, she *needed* the truth, and she also *needed* to make a point.

As they neared the door, Fyrn set to work clearing any protective spells on the entrance. He made short work of them—in seconds, small puffs of smoke wafted out of the keyholes. When he had finished, he gave a curt nod toward the door.

Now or never.

Victoria gestured for them to wait outside and twisted the magnificent red door's elaborate golden knob.

"We're coming with you," Diesel whispered.

"This is a solo gig. Stay hidden."

"Victoria, she's dangerous."

"So am I," Victoria said with a smirk. Not eager to debate it further, she slipped into the room and shut the door behind her.

She pressed her back against the closed door and surveyed the scene, looking for traps or guards.

All was silent.

In fact, the utterly quiet bedroom reminded Victoria of a museum, maybe one of the classy ones she saw in documentaries at school, like the Louvre. A high school gymnasium could have fit in the enormous round room. Elaborate white columns dotted the space every ten feet or so and pedestals sat between them, holding a crystal chalices or jewelry or other shiny things.

In the center of the room sat a round bed draped in a thick crimson blanket. The fabric rose and fell gently as the sleeping figure in its center breathed.

Victoria eyed the rest of the room one last time to check for anyone who might interrupt her. A doorway on the far side probably led to a bathroom of some sort, but there were no other entrances or exits beside the door through which she had just come.

She crept across the white marble floor, careful not to make a peep. The whole point of this exercise was to show the queen how close she could get without killing her outright.

A show of force. A *creepy* show of force, maybe, but it was the only way she would get the truth out of this woman.

From the head of the bed, Victoria slowly circled it. She was less careful to be quiet now that she was where she wanted to be.

When she rounded the headboard, the queen's eyes were already open. The regal woman watched Victoria, body tense even though she didn't move a muscle. They studied each other for a moment, each waiting for the other to strike. Victoria was prepared to summon her shield if need be, since she had no intention of hurting the queen.

Victoria was merely here to talk.

"If you're going to kill me, let's get on with it," the queen said.

Victoria almost laughed. "Do you want me to kill you?"

"Of course not, but that's why you're here. Let's not drag it out."

Victoria shook her head. "I won't kill you unless you make me."

The queen let out a dry laugh. "What do you want? Money? Was the Rhazdon Artifact not enough for you?"

"You and I both know I don't have it yet. You sent me to kill that sphinx without everything I needed. You lied to me about the one thing that would have truly helped."

Queen Angelique raised an elegant eyebrow. "And that was?"

"The testimony of the person who came back from an encounter with the sphinx. The one person who knows why it needs the dark magic so badly."

The queen sat up in her beautiful bed, but she didn't speak. Victoria remained tense and ready to deflect a blow if she had to.

"It's you, isn't it? The survivor?" Victoria pressed.

At first the queen didn't move, but slowly she nodded.

"Why didn't you tell me? All you had to do was talk a little more. You had shared so much already."

The queen cast her gaze briefly to the floor, and the sudden realization sank in so deeply it almost hurt.

Victoria clenched her fist, thoroughly pissed off as she put the last piece in place. "You thought it would kill us. It was your own version of an execution, except with no blood on your hands."

"It gave the people hope," Queen Angelique said softly.

"Just tell me how to kill it and they'll get more than hope. They'll be free."

"Will they?" The queen glared at Victoria, her demeanor shifting to righteous anger. "You'll come back, Victoria. You'll want someone to sacrifice to merge with it. And why stop with one soul when you can take them all? Strength of body. Strength of heart. Strength of mind. Getting that Rhazdon Artifact will make you invincible, and being a Rhazdon host will make you bloodthirsty. No, it was better that the sphinx take you, even if it meant we were trapped longer. Even if it meant we were trapped *forever*."

"And those packs you gave us? Was that to allay suspicion?"

The queen's shoulders drooped. "More like a way to assuage my guilt, honestly."

"Oh, *now* you're honest."

The queen glared at Victoria, taking the bait. "Why wouldn't I be? Only one of us is leaving this room."

"I won't attack unless you do. I'm not here to fight you, Angelique. I'm here to make a point."

"It's Queen—"

"I don't give a shit about your title."

The queen frowned but didn't speak, instead resting her hands in her lap as she calmly waited for her execution.

Victoria resisted the impulse to pace the room to vent her anger. "I won't call you 'Queen.' Not right now. Not when you're in your nightgown, wondering if you'll survive an encounter with someone—some*thing*—you were raised to hate. Whether you like it or not we're equals, if only for the moment. And my point is this, Angelique... I *could* kill you. I *could* destroy everything you love. I could let the dark magic in my Rhazdon Artifact corrupt me, let it rule me, *but I don't want to.* All I'm trying to do is protect my home, same as you. Even if you hate what I am, can you at least meet me halfway and see what I'm trying to accomplish?"

Angelique's red lips parted slightly, and she seemed to struggle to speak. "What kind of Rhazdon host are you?"

"The best kind," Victoria said before she could help herself. She could never resist snark when someone lobbed a stupid question at her. It was too easy.

Angelique slipped out of bed, cautiously standing as she studied Victoria. "You're right. Back when my elder sister was alive and I could be reckless—back when I didn't ever expect to need to stay alive to rule—I went on the hunting party that mapped the safe tunnel to the inner lair, but our party was ambushed by that *thing*. It broke down the passageway's walls, which I didn't think was even possible. Nothing should be able to break the charms on our tunnels, not even centuries of neglect and a powerful sphinx."

Victoria nodded, thinking about the hole in the tunnel where she had wounded the sphinx. It made sense now—

that was an old hole, likely the one through which the beast had attacked Angelique's group. "How did you survive?"

"Talent and stubbornness. I pretty much crawled back with my injuries, but I hurt the monster enough to get away. Its eyes are its weakest point."

Victoria shook her head. "I disagree. It's the neck."

Angelique's eyes widened. "You saw it again, didn't you? You faced it and lived?"

"Three times now," Victoria said, putting a hand on her hip to drive home the point.

To her credit, Angelique smiled. "You keep surprising me, Victoria."

Victoria gave a mock bow, not wanting to take her eyes off the monarch in case it was a ploy to get her to lower her guard. "I still need to know why it craves the dark magic in the Rhazdon Artifact."

"Fuel," Angelique said without pausing this time, evidently more willing to open up now that she and Victoria had been talking for a while. "It's our theory that the dark magic provides the power it needs to create the confusing hellscape of the inner and outer lairs. Without the Rhazdon Artifact nearby, it effectively has no home in which to hide."

"And we can flush it out," Victoria finished.

Angelique nodded.

"Good. I think I have what I need. Thank you." With that, Victoria headed for the door.

"Just like that? You're leaving?" Angelique asked.

Victoria hesitated, eyes darting between the door and the monarch as she tried to find what she was missing in the situation. "Yes?"

"You break into my room and finally give me the missing pieces of the puzzle to kill this monster, and you think I'm not going to take my army to finish the job?"

Victoria stood up straight, not entirely sure if she liked the idea of a woman she didn't fully trust fighting with her. However, more soldiers were always welcome in a fight against something as massive and deadly as the sphinx.

It was a toss-up, really.

The queen arched her back. "We have two hours until morning. I'll ready my soldiers by then, and we'll meet you in the tunnels outside the city. In the meantime, I suggest you get some sleep." The queen paused, eyeing Victoria. "If that's something you Rhazdon hosts do."

Victoria huffed and left the room without another word, not entirely sure if her plan had worked successfully or if she had merely complicated things for herself.

In the end, all that mattered was she had gotten the information she needed. *So, a win I guess?*

Ugh.

When the door shut behind her, she scanned the empty hallway in search of her friends. She panicked for a moment, wondering if the guards had found them, but she knew better. They were cloaked in one of Fyrn's spells. She gave the thumbs-up, their signal, and all three of them appeared, seemingly out of thin air. Styx flitted down to her from the ceiling, his wings humming as he neared.

"Well, things just got interesting," she confessed.

CHAPTER TWENTY-THREE

"What part of 'she's going to kill me, damn it' aren't you getting, V?" Audrey paced the tunnels outside of Lochrose City proper, hand in her hair as she tried to process this latest turn of events.

Diesel had taken the opportunity to go resupply, and gluttonous little Styx had joined him. Victoria had urged them to return quickly in case they wanted to move without the queen and her army.

As it stood, they had yet to decide on a plan.

Victoria groaned and leaned against a nearby wall. "That thing has nearly eaten us three times now. We need the help. Can you shift, at least until the fighting starts? I doubt they'll notice your tiara in the heat of battle."

"They'll notice," Fyrn said in his gravelly voice.

"Thanks. *Big* help," Victoria said dryly.

Fyrn shrugged. "It's the truth. When we face the sphinx, we must be focused on the fight with it and not turn on each other. If they see an Atlantean suddenly in their midst, they will attack first and ask questions later. Everyone will die."

Audrey sighed. Fair point. She continued pacing, mind racing for answers.

In her peripheral vision, something darted across a wall of gemstones. She hesitated, watching out of the corner of her eye, and a second figure temporarily blocked the glow from the stones. The shadows crouched as though trying to remain unseen, and Audrey stiffened.

Victoria seemed to notice a shift, as did Fyrn. All of them tensed, and Audrey reached a hand into her pocket. If she had already been spotted by the Lochrosian army, shifting now wouldn't do any good.

She cursed herself. In her attempt to preserve her energy, she had waited to shift until the last moment. Rookie move. She should have shifted the moment Victoria told her what had happened, should have…

Well, she hadn't. Only that mattered, and now she had to face the consequences, whatever they were.

Something in the tunnel roared, familiar and yet out of place at the same time. The sound struck an almost nostalgic chord in Audrey's heart, and it took a moment to recognize the sound.

The roar of an orc, a sound she had often heard on the Berserk field.

Out of the shadows stormed at least a dozen elves and orcs wearing the dark uniforms Audrey had seen on a few of the mercenaries who now enforced Luak's growing rule over Fairhaven. They raced toward the small group, the Light Elves' skin glowing with runes as they prepared to attack.

"I guess they want to die today," Audrey said, grip tightening on the crystal.

Audrey didn't wait for Victoria or Fyrn. She lifted her hand and fired a bolt of brilliant white light at the ambush, frying two of the mercenaries mid-stride. White light haloed their bodies as they hovered in midair, locked in place by her magic. When she released them they fell over, smoking.

The second wave of fighters charged.

Idiots. They hadn't even looked at their fallen companions to realize what would happen to them.

As the white light burst from her body, Audrey savored how easily it came. The more she practiced, the less of her own energy each bolt took. She was grateful to have the upper hand for once and not be at an attacker's mercy like she had been with General Cato.

Never again. Not her.

She shot a final bolt into the chest of the last orc, who froze and fell over backward as though he had been tazed.

"Help! Stop this! I command you to stop!" a woman screamed from nearby.

Audrey's ears perked as she tried to find the sound, only to realize it came from behind them. She spun to find a lone Light Elf with a woman in his arms, his glowing hand pressed to her head.

Queen Angelique of Lochrose. She wore black leather armor and a golden cloak, her hair braided and pinned behind her head. Hands raised and eyes wide, it seemed like she had been caught completely off-guard.

"Fuuuuuck," Victoria said under her breath.

"Move one inch and she dies," the mercenary spat. He

wrestled to get a better grip on the woman in his arms, careful to use her as a shield to protect his body.

"What do you want?" Victoria asked.

"You and her." The Light Elf nodded toward Audrey.

"No," Victoria said flatly.

The light in the elf's palm grew brighter, and the queen winced. He sneered. "Try your answer again."

Fyrn shifted his weight, his hands wrapped around his staff as he eyed the mercenary.

"Don't think about it, old man," the Light Elf said.

Fyrn merely narrowed his eyes in warning. Whatever happened, this would not end well for the mercenary.

Audrey scanned the area behind him, wondering if he had more backup. It seemed as though his force had separated at some point to attack from both sides, and corpses lay along the floor behind the Light Elf. Victoria and Fyrn had covered their attack and come out on top.

A familiar face lay among the dead mercenaries, but it took a moment for her to recognize the wizard she had once met on top of the Fairhaven palace's balcony. "Is that—"

The Light Elf chanced a quick glance to the side, and his wicked sneer widened. "The late, great King Bornt."

The king sprawled on the ground, the veins in his face bright purple as he stared vacantly at the ceiling. Instead of his usual cloak and elegant clothes, he wore only a brown tunic and tattered, stained paints. Blood trickled out of the side of his mouth.

"Victoria, you killed the damn king!" Audrey shouted.

"It wasn't me!"

"Shut up, both of you!" the Light Elf snapped.

"What did you do to Bornt?" Victoria demanded.

"You'll find out if you don't come with me, girl."

As he shifted his weight, hand still sizzling against Queen Angelique's temple, Audrey got a clear shot at his head. He seemed more focused on Victoria and Fyrn and kept slowly shifting toward them.

Big mistake.

Audrey had a good chunk of his exposed head to aim at, and her aim had improved significantly since her target practice in Atlantis. She gently lifted a finger in such a way that it would be hidden from the mercenary until the last moment.

As the queen's struggling eased, her gaze rested on Audrey. It flitted from Audrey's face to the tiara on her head, and her eyes widened instantly with recognition.

Audrey had a choice, and she didn't like either outcome. Either she let the Light Elf kill the queen, which would mean an army came after them for vengeance, or she would kill the attacker and probably die instantly regardless because she was Atlantean.

She sighed. Damn ethics.

Quick as a whip, she fired a white bolt of light at the mercenary. The queen screamed, but the jolt of energy sailed like a bullet clear through the elf's skull.

Still tense with fear, the queen swayed as the Light Elf fell to the ground in a sizzling heap.

Queen Angelique swiveled her head from the Light Elf to Audrey and back as though unable to process what had happened. "You saved me."

"You're welcome," Audrey muttered, ready to run if she

had to. Victoria tensed as well, and Fyrn lifted his staff to show he, too, was ready for battle.

"But you're Atlantean," Queen Angelique said softly.

"And *you* were supposed to have fighting skills," Victoria interrupted, likely to change the subject.

Not that it would do any good.

Queen Angelique blinked herself out of her reverie and shot a stern look at Victoria. "I'll have you know the 'mind meld' spell is exceedingly difficult. It takes years of mastery, and yes, perhaps some of my other skills have suffered. I don't see *you* reading minds, Host. Besides, I came to see if you were ready to leave for the sphinx, not to engage in a battle outside my front door!"

"Don't you have guards?"

"Killed by those men who no doubt chased you down here, so watch your tone! Those were good wizards with families! With children!"

Victoria's shoulders relaxed, and her expression softened. "I'm sorry you lost some of your own. We would have helped if we could."

"I know." The queen absently adjusted her armor, taking a step back as she glared at Audrey.

"Are you going to kill me?" Audrey asked, ready to fight if need be.

The queen hesitated as if considering the option. "Not today."

"Not ever," Victoria barked. The queen straightened and opened her mouth to protest, but Victoria didn't let her say a word. "If you attack her, you attack me. And I promise you, Queen Angelique, you do *not* want to attack me."

To Audrey's surprise, a small smile played at the queen's lips. "You're right, Host. I don't."

With that, the queen turned toward one of the disguised side tunnels and disappeared into the rocky wall.

Seconds later, Diesel popped out of the same tunnel and stopped dead in his tracks, eyes scanning the bodies littered across the ground. "What did I miss?"

CHAPTER TWENTY-FOUR

Victoria walked shoulder to shoulder with the queen, but she couldn't help feeling that the tense alliance might backfire at any moment.

Audrey walked ahead of her, with Diesel and Fyrn behind her to protect her back—not that it stopped the glares. Victoria was fairly sure the soldiers scowled at Audrey with all the hatred they could muster. She imagined they all wished they could unsheathe their wands and rip her apart.

Over Victoria's dead body.

The thought of dead bodies reminded her of the king's corpse among the others, and suddenly the saying had more meaning. He had probably tried to flee during the battle, and the mercenary had stabbed him in the back.

Alone, scared, and lost. What a horrible way to go.

Victoria shook the thought from her mind. They were on a warpath, and she needed to focus.

As was typical for the wizard tunnels, Victoria felt as though she blinked and they were suddenly at a second entrance tunnel to the inner lair. This one was supposed to be better than the last, with a more secure vantage point.

It annoyed her that Angelique had sent her to the tunnel where the queen herself had nearly died, but she tried to leave it in the past.

After all, Angelique wasn't trying to kill her anymore.

Probably.

While the soldiers waited in the back with Fyrn, Audrey, and Diesel, Victoria and Angelique crept to the edge of the tunnel and peered into the cavern. This entrance had a much better perspective than their last access point to the inner lair, one that brought them closer to both the pedestal and the ground.

"If only we had bait," the queen muttered.

"Bait?" Victoria asked, voice hushed.

Angelique nodded. "Something the creature couldn't resist. Something we could use to lure it away from the Rhazdon Artifact."

With a horrifying pang, Victoria looked over her shoulder at Audrey. Audrey perked up and almost instantly narrowed her eyes, their universal expression for, *Stop what you're thinking right now.*

Styx flitted over and landed on Victoria's shoulder as her plan began to form.

Man, Audrey was going to be *pissed.*

CHAPTER TWENTY-FIVE

P erched at the edge of the tunnel, Audrey took a deep breath. She tensed herself to run, absolutely astonished at what she was about to do.

Namely, who she was about to trust.

"Are you sure about this, V?" Audrey asked, without glancing over her shoulder at the horde of wizards who all wanted her dead.

"Should you die, I will avenge you in a heroic fashion."

Audrey glared at her friend. "I'm not joking around here."

Victoria sighed, equally tense. "I know you don't like the idea of trusting them." She nodded back at the queen and her four dozen elite soldiers, all of whom knelt as though they were in a race against each other, merely waiting for the starting gun.

"Yeah, that sums it up pretty well."

"Diesel and Fyrn will also be out there. The sphinx wants you, Audrey, and it's going to go after you first regardless. Everyone is going to be looking out for you, trying to confuse and overwhelm it."

"Everyone but you."

Victoria set a comforting arm on Audrey's shoulder, and Audrey regretted her outburst almost instantly.

They didn't need to say anything, but Audrey did anyway. "I'm sorry. I know you have the hardest job. *You're* going for the kill."

"The sphinx will not kill you, Audrey. I'll make sure of it."

"What about the wizards back there? They want to."

"They won't. They don't want to go to war with me."

Audrey nearly blew a raspberry. "Do they know you were a cashier at a grocery store? Scary things, plastic bags."

Victoria chuckled. "That's not who I am anymore, is it?"

Audrey smiled. "No, I guess not. You're a big bad host."

"As are you, Audrey. The Lochrosians might not want to go to war with me, but they also don't want this sphinx down here anymore. They'll stay on task. Don't worry. I don't want to lose you, and I wouldn't ask you to do this without knowing you can pull it off. When you go out there I'm going to do everything in my power to keep you safe, even if you can't see me."

"Good, because if I die I'm going to haunt the ever-loving *fuck* out of you."

With that, Audrey bolted down the path toward the beast's inner lair, putting all her trust in the best friend she had followed into the depths of the Earth time and time again.

The sphinx roared from somewhere deep within the

cavern, and Audrey set her face in grim determination as it descended upon her. She would likely have to focus all her energy on running, but she would get in as many shots at the massive beast as she could.

After all, she couldn't let Victoria have *all* the fun.

It was chaos.

Fyrn raced along the edges of the battle as the sphinx snapped at the soldiers surrounding its feet. One eye still swollen shut from Victoria's attack, the monster kept looking for Audrey in the chaos of wizards and spells blasting at its face.

In its fury, the massive creature did almost nothing but scream. The thundering shrieks shook the walls, dislodging boulders that rolled into the cavern. Its tail and wings thrashed, knocking stalactites to the ground and flattening anything beneath its feet.

Several wizards lay dead, giant gashes in their torsos or whole limbs missing from the rampage. Regardless, the small army soldiered on. With every blow, the creature protected its neck either by tucking its chin toward its chest or blatantly holding up a claw.

Despite their best efforts and several dead soldiers, the sphinx had yet to give even an inch.

Fyrn muttered an ancient spell, one he hadn't been able to use in decades because it was too powerful, and aimed his staff at the creature's face. Brilliant red light shot from the crystal in its tip like a supernova exploding through the sky, and it smacked perfectly against the sphinx's temple.

Eyes squeezed shut, body tensing, back arched, the monster howled in pain. The blood red light of Fyrn's spell burrowed beneath its skin, and boils festered instantly around its face. Flailing, the creature fell back against the cliff wall. The cavern shook with the thunderous impact.

In its agony, the sphinx lifted one palm to its face and exposed the all-too-vulnerable neck.

This was Victoria's game now. They had set the stage, but it was up to her to deal the final blow.

CHAPTER TWENTY-SIX

Victoria skidded on the ground, ducking a swipe from the monster's claw by inches. She rolled, checking the sphinx to get a feel for its focus, but it didn't notice her.

Not far ahead, the thin streams of golden light she had been eyeing for so long were finally within reach. The beams illuminated a single pillar, on which sat the tiniest figurine she had ever seen. The small bear had been carved from a dark stone and had red gemstone eyes that glimmered in the light.

Finally.

She snatched it off the pedestal, and the ground beneath her shook. At first she thought perhaps it was a trap, one she had triggered when she moved the Rhazdon Artifact, but then she realized the thundering earthquake was coming from behind her.

They were footsteps.

The sphinx bared its teeth as it charged her, boils covering its once-smooth face and one eye swollen shut.

God, this thing was *ugly*.

Victoria barely had time to roll out of the way. It bit into the rock behind her, its massive jaws crunching through the stone as though it were paper.

Victoria scrambled to her feet and stuffed the Rhazdon Artifact in her pocket. Audrey and Fyrn nursed an injured Diesel. She waved them on, urging them to get to higher ground, but Audrey ran toward her.

The sphinx's massive wings stretched out as it growled, ready to pounce on her, and the wings crashed into the walls around it. Boulders fell from the cave walls high above, smashing against the ground. Every impact threw Victoria off balance, and it was all she could do to stay on her feet.

Audrey skidded to a halt, trying to dodge the rocks as they fell. To her horror, Victoria saw one falling directly for Audrey, which she didn't seem to see. Over the thundering crash of the cave-in, she couldn't yell for her friend's attention.

No. No!

In a last-minute move inspired by panic and desperation, Victoria threw her shield at Audrey. The flat face of the magical shield hit Audrey hard enough to knock her out of range even as the sphinx's paw landed hard on Victoria's leg. The claw dug into her and searing pain ripped up her thigh. She couldn't suppress the scream that erupted from her chest.

The rocks began to pile up, and she hoped against hope that her shield had saved Audrey. All the Rhazdon Artifacts in the world would mean nothing if even one of them cost her the life of someone she loved.

Audrey's arms were about to give out. Hips on the ground, she heaved upward in a pathetic attempt at a pushup while she tried to stand. At first she thought maybe her legs were crushed, trapped beneath one of the boulders., but then she realized she was pinned beneath Victoria's shield.

Audrey lifted the shield as best she could, since her muscles weren't as accustomed to the heavy thing as Victoria's. When she finally wrestled free of it, she scanned the rubble. The alcove that had held the pedestal was now filled with stones. Audrey couldn't even see the rays of light anymore.

"Victoria!" Audrey began to scrape at the massive pile of rocks, as if that would do anything. Not a single one moved.

A warm hand rested on her shoulder, and she spun to find Fyrn. Behind him the queen's army nursed their wounds, and one of their medics was healing Diesel. He sucked in a sharp breath as the gaping hole in his shoulder closed.

"Fyrn, we have to help," Audrey said, trying again to dig through the rocks.

"This is still the sphinx's cave, Audrey. There's not a thing we can do to get through the rock until she kills it."

"You're going to give up, just like that?"

The old wizard chuckled. "Don't be ridiculous. I'm probably more stubborn than you are."

Audrey sniffled in gratitude, utterly unwilling to admit she had been close to tears. "Nowhere close."

Utterly exhausted from the battle, Audrey knew she

didn't have the energy left for any more of her Atlantean attacks. Instead, she resumed digging while he aimed spell after spell at the wall. A moment later Diesel joined them, and the trio did what they could.

On the other side of the wall, Victoria wrestled for her life.

The sphinx batted her around like a plaything, but thanks to her healing ability she was nearly back to peak health. It snarled, tail curling like a cat's.

As the final twinge of her latest injury faded, she cleared her mind and summoned her shield to her. She waited for the familiar weight in her palm, and smiled gratefully when it came.

The creature growled, the low click in the back of its throat almost a purr as it crouched for another attack. Shield now in hand, she lifted it seconds before the monster pounced. Claws scraped across the metal shield, not even denting the magical metal.

Thwarted, the sphinx paced around the alcove, barely large enough to fit. It ducked its head several times as it sized her up, the one good eye roaming Victoria's body as it no doubt searched for weaknesses.

Adrenaline poured through every vein in Victoria's body. Despite her exhaustion from the ordeal in Lochrose, she was ready for this. She would fight till her last breath if she had to, in order to kill this thing.

The sphinx would die tonight.

She dismissed her shield and instead summoned a sword. Apparently sensing a vulnerability, the creature lunged and bit at her head. Victoria ducked the fatal blow and dug her sword deep into its ankle. The creature teetered, limping as blood gushed from the wound.

They danced like this for what felt like ages. With every swing of her blade, Victoria's shoulders slouched a little more. With every roar from the monster, her ears rang a little louder. With every scrape of claws along the rock, fatigue ate a little more into Victoria's brain.

She was nearing her limit.

The beast's teeth and claws caught her time and time again. The claws ripped off her sleeves and tore a gash in her abdomen. A trail of blood down her temple nearly obscured her vision several times. With each passing second, her defenses got worse.

To her horror, Victoria was losing.

"You are *mine*," the monster hissed.

"I like being single," she said, her voice rough and crackly. "I think we should just stay friends."

It frowned and chomped at her head, and she barely rolled out of the way in time. Through sheer will, she managed to keep her sword in her hand.

Panting, aching, her energy fading fast, Victoria stared at the creature. It coiled as if about to land its death strike, and Victoria wondered if this was how she would die.

Bloody.

Beaten.

Alone.

Like King Bornt.

Luak's doing, no doubt. He had battered Fairhaven into submission and enslaved its ruler out of spite. Luak was at the center of all of this. All the pain, all the hatred, and all the death.

The hate and rage for everything Luak had done lit a fire within her she had thought could shine no brighter.

Her parents hadn't died for her to end up as a sphinx's dinner. Fairhaven would never succumb to a monster like Luak. Innocent humans and Oricerans alike would no longer die simply because Luak wanted something from them.

And she, Victoria Brie, would not die today.

The coiled sphinx attacked with all the ferocity of a lion, and Victoria was ready. She aimed her sword at the monster's exposed neck and, wounded as it was, the sphinx never saw it coming.

The blade dug in all the way to the hilt, and the monster gurgled as blood pooled in its mouth. It fell to the ground with a crash, and Victoria barely got out of the way.

Even in its death throes the creature tried to rip into her, but its claws retracted involuntarily. Slowly, agonizingly, the life faded from its eyes.

It could no longer hurt anyone.

Exhausted and not quite thinking straight, Victoria lifted the little figurine and studied it. All this blood, all this danger for something so small. She held it to her exposed abdomen, grateful this was over.

As the sphinx's head slumped to the ground and it finally died, an excruciating pain tore through her body. Tears burned in her eyes. She fell to her knees, unable to stem the scream that burst from her. Her body convulsed, and she fell backward as the world rumbled around her. It was as though the rocks in the ceiling above were tumbling toward her, and she welcomed death if it would only stop this pain.

———

Two hands lifted her into a soft and warm lap. Victoria tried to open her eyes, but everything hurt.

Why do I hurt so much? She shouldn't hurt at all, not with the Rhazdon Artifact in her arm. It could heal her.

"Victoria?" an echoing voice asked.

Shit, had the sphinx learned her name?

Her pain-addled mind took a moment to remember that the sphinx was dead. Someone else was calling her. She struggled to open her eyes, but she couldn't. She rested her head against whoever held her and let the darkness take her.

CHAPTER TWENTY-SEVEN

V ictoria had no idea how long she slept, but she loved every minute of it.

When she finally woke, she was in an ornate bed similar to the queen's. Though her room was smaller, the round design reminded her very much of the room she had snuck into not that long ago.

She sat up, scanning the room for clues as the sheer golden blanket fell down her torso. Two chairs flanked a massive window overlooking the golden Lochrose City courtyard. A green gown had been draped over one chair, while pants and a white shirt reposed, neatly folded, in the seat of the other.

Her head ached, and she willed her magic to cure it. The flow of energy from her Rhazdon Artifact obeyed, and the pain slowly ebbed.

"Now you've done it," Shiloh said, suddenly standing behind her.

Victoria only jumped a little, and she was too tired to care about his attitude. "What did I do?"

"We have company," he said with a nod to the window. "Forever."

Victoria followed his gaze to find an elvish woman standing by the window. Her hand rested against the pane, and the faint outline of the city beyond was visible through the ghostly silhouette of her wiry frame.

"It's been so long," the light elf said softly.

"What's your name?" Victoria stood, noting that she was dressed in a nightgown. Since she had a Rhazdon ghost to tend to, she chose not to question who had changed her clothes just then.

The elf spun on her heel and smiled warmly, caringly. "Elle. I'm so glad you found me. That dumb cat licked my Artifact for centuries. *Licked* it, Victoria! I wanted to *kill it*!"

For a terrifying instant the elf's sweet face twisted in a horrifyingly distorted expression rife with anger and rage. Exaggerated wrinkles covered her temples and cheeks, and jagged teeth protruded suddenly from her mouth. Her eyes went blood-red, and she grew a foot taller.

As quickly as she had gone evil, the little elf was sweet and small again. "We're going to be great friends!"

Victoria froze, shocked and not quite sure how to respond to the outburst. "Uh huh."

The elf giggled and disappeared into thin air. With a bored sigh, Shiloh did the same.

Victoria absently scratched her chest as she stared out the window. Her finger touched a sensitive area, and she glanced down at a few black swirls of a tattoo she had never gotten.

Curious and a bit concerned what the second Rhazdon Artifact had done to her, she unbuttoned the top of her gown and raced over to the mirror. The outline of a tribal-style bear was now tattooed across her torso in colorful swirls. In its center was the figurine, fused to her body.

She rolled up the sleeve on her right arm and examined both the new tattoo and the dagger.

Wow. She had done it. She had really done it.

With these Rhazdon Artifacts, she could finally defeat Luak. And boy, did that asshole have it coming.

CHAPTER TWENTY-EIGHT

Despite promising no payment besides the Rhazdon Artifact, Queen Angelique had thrown Victoria and her friends a celebration. They experienced the full honors of Lochrosian heroes, including medals, flower petals, and a spell-generated twenty-one-gun salute.

Victoria had hated most of it, because the fanfare made her nervous. At any moment someone could jump out of the crowd and attack. She was, after all, a Rhazdon host, and more than one grizzled wizard had reached for his wand as she passed.

Audrey, though, had had a much worse time of it. Many of the civilians glared at her tiara, and she had never gone anywhere without a suspiciously observant entourage.

But they had suffered through it to make Angelique happy, which honestly surprised Victoria. At some point in the battle their precarious truce had become an alliance.

Thank goodness it was over.

With a bored sigh, Victoria tapped her thumbs together.

She and Fyrn were waiting in a penthouse suite in New York City.

She'd had one more job to do before she took on Luak head-to-head.

She and Fyrn sat in silence, each keeping their eye on the hotel room's door. Any minute now the senior official who oversaw the division in charge of "requesting" magical help would walk into his penthouse suite and get a very nasty surprise.

Victoria wasn't going to kill him, but she wouldn't mind breaking a few of his bones. No one threatened her people, and blackmailing Fyrn was equivalent to blackmailing *her*.

And she didn't take kindly to threats.

The door finally swung open, and Victoria stood without a sound. In a few easy steps she ducked behind it, so as to remain hidden while the man entered.

A bald man in a black suit stopped after just a few steps and his head jerked toward the still-seated Fyrn. Apparently he took a few moments to evaluate his life choices, because there was a delay before he tried to flee.

Before he could make it into the hallway, Victoria used her newfound strength to force the door closed. It slammed so hard the wall shook, and she hid a grimace. It would take time to explore the bear figurine's power, but this would do for now.

Not entirely concerned with the man's wellbeing, Victoria lifted him and threw him backward. He landed on his ass and skidded as though she had thrown a pillow and not a full-grown man.

Damn, this strength was wonderful. While she didn't understand why a petite elf like Elle was tied to the bear, she was sure she would find out eventually. And if Shiloh's story was any indication, it would not be a pleasant chat.

"You're going to listen very closely," Fyrn snapped. He tapped his staff against the blue carpet and the crystal glowed to life.

"Y-you can't hurt me. I could expose Fairhaven and all the magical cities. I could—"

"You could try shutting your mouth," Victoria interrupted.

The bald man turned his attention toward her. "You don't know the trouble you just got yourself into. You—"

Victoria summoned her blade out of thin air, and the man squeaked.

He squeaked.

Victoria couldn't believe this was the man in charge of magical affairs, but if he were coward enough to blackmail Fyrn and then hide, she supposed she shouldn't be surprised.

"Do you know what I am?" Victoria asked.

Fyrn shot her a warning glare, but she knew what she was doing. After dealing with the Lochrosian Queen, Victoria could handle this little extortionist.

"No," the man admitted.

"I'm a very bad enemy to have. I'm not entirely human anymore, and quite frankly, I don't like you. If you blackmail anyone with the threat of exposing Fairhaven again, you won't live long enough to follow through. Are we clear?"

He gulped so loudly she heard him swallow. That was answer enough for her.

Satisfied, she nodded to Fyrn and gestured toward the door. "Shall we?"

The old wizard frowned, but obliged her. When the door had shut behind them, he leaned in and whispered, "Laid it on a little thick, didn't you?"

She shrugged. "He deserved it."

"Can't fault you there."

They headed toward the taxi waiting for them in the back alley. Thanks to Fyrn's magic, any cameras that picked up their images would see only their glamours: two kangaroos bouncing through the hall.

Victoria grinned. Magic was a beautiful thing.

End of Book Three.
Victoria & Audrey return in Nightfall (Fairhaven Chronicles #4), which is available now at Amazon and through Kindle Unlimited.

Busy time of year for everyone. Good for you for de-stressing with a good story! A little magic always helps me unwind and The Fairhaven Chronicles takes me away to a fun adventure. Books are a great way to take a break from relatives too.

The holidays do approach and there's a lot of planning going on to make sure everyone catches a plane or the guest room is clean or shopping, shopping, shopping. I have a tradition from Chicago that I've missed and look forward to reinstating when I get back there next year. It's more suited for that kind of place – a city with a lot of great transportation – tends to lend itself to a population that moves around a lot and is always on the go.

Thing is, a lot of those same people didn't have a place to go for Thanksgiving dinner. Home was too far away or there weren't any relatives. So, my first year in Chicago I put out the word that I was having a potluck Thanksgiving, all were welcome to put their feet under my small, glass topped table in my tiny kitchen. That Thursday, the kitchen was full and I only knew one of the faces – the offspring. The rest were newcomers and it was one of the best times I ever had.

After that, I started doing it for every holiday. Now, keep in mind that my kitchen was so small that to get something out of the oven, everyone on one side of this tiny table that I found in an alley had to get up and move out of the way. And yet, every holiday the place was full – there was an Easter where I had to borrow chairs and dishes from the neighbor upstairs. Word got around that there was always a seat available at Martha's. This was taking place against the backdrop of the Great Recession and I look back now and wonder how I was able to afford the food every year. There was a year where someone got a free turkey from their job and that helped out a lot. Still, it all came together every time and there was everyone's favorite and leftovers and a lot of laughter around that table. These are some of my best memories.

It didn't make a difference about the surroundings – the couch was used and lovingly referred to as the spoon because of the way it curved in the middle, the TV was a 24" (but color!) and the dishes were Corelle and all anyone talks about to this day is how much fun they had with each other. In the end, that's all that matters – the connections we make. Happy Thanksgiving everyone!

Thank you for reading the Fairhaven Chronicles!

(And making it through Martha's author notes as she believes she was able to author note block me. Since you are reading this note, she failed. If you are not reading this note, she succeeded – not that you would know that since you aren't reading these notes right now.)

How is that for logic?

I've decided that I hope to provide a little insight on some of the challenges and wins of becoming a small indie publisher (as opposed to an indie author publishing) during these Publisher notes.

Right now, my company LMBPN is focused on *not* adding additional authors so as we are fixing two important challenges – art and marketing. On the art side, I've engaged some of our artists and made sure that we are supporting them appropriately so that our pipeline (which can be a little wild and difficult from time to time) doesn't overcome their ability to get out a quality cover without ripping out their hair.

Because an artist with most of their hair gone is a very sad head to see.

At times, you work with an artist who is so amazing, you keep wanting to place them on another project, and another, and another and so on. However, I did this recently when I spread an artist too thin and gummed up the works on other projects with a 'pet project' 3d troll.

To be fair to me, both myself and the artist didn't know how long it would take to do a troll in 3d. I have since learned that you need to add the word *incredibly* in front of *long* when discussing 3d projects. Especially projects with hair.

Either way, the 3d troll caused a domino effect to miss another book cover finishing and *DAMN* - release date destroyed for another author.

Art is a major issue with production, and at the speed we are producing, it is also a major expense. LMBPN Publishing is working to create high-quality covers (that match the genre) while pulling down the expense if possible.

Our second pillar of effort in my company is related to marketing more effectively. I'm talking about becoming better with ads (Facebook, Bookbub, and Amazon Marketing Services), using email more effectively and creating word-of-mouth among happy readers.

This challenge might be a harder nut to crack. We shall see.

Either way, when we fix the marketing issue, I will be able to help ALL of the authors in our group by spreading the cheer of their books and increase the series sales, magnifying their take home as well.

That will be a good day, for sure.

In another note, many of the LMBPN collaboration authors are joining the Science Fiction and Fantasy Writers of America group (which is open to anyone world-wide) and our first meeting will be in May.

Traditional Writers? Meet Indie Writers… Indie Writers, meet Traditional. I know SFWA has been open to Indie writers for a while, but if I can swing it, I hope 20 of us will join the meeting this year, and move it to 50 next year and do one of those 'hear us roar' things. Probably not, authors are a rather introverted group, so it might be more of a 'we are indie, hear us typing on our laptops while we hide in our rooms' sort of thing.

We shall see.

As the end of the year comes up, I wish you and your family whether they be by birth, or friendship or closeness, the very best holidays.

Ad Aeternitatem,
Michael

OTHER SERIES IN THE ORICERAN
UNIVERSE:

THE DANIEL CODEX SERIES
I FEAR NO EVIL
THE UNBELIEVABLE MR. BROWNSTONE
ALISON BROWNSTONE
SCHOOL OF NECESSARY MAGIC
SCHOOL OF NECESSARY MAGIC: RAINE CAMPBELL
FEDERAL AGENTS OF MAGIC
SCIONS OF MAGIC
THE LEIRA CHRONICLES
REWRITING JUSTICE
THE KACY CHRONICLES
MIDWEST MAGIC CHRONICLES
SOUL STONE MAGE
THE FAIRHAVEN CHRONICLES

OTHER BOOKS BY JUDITH BERENS

CONNECT WITH THE AUTHORS

Martha Carr Social

Website:
http://www.marthacarr.com

Facebook:
https://www.facebook.com/groups/MarthaCarrFans/

https://www.facebook.com/terranavisuniverse/

Michael Anderle Social

Michael Anderle Social
Website:
http://www.lmbpn.com

Email List:
http://lmbpn.com/email/

Facebook
https://www.facebook.com/TheKurtherianGambitBooks/